FROM THE LIBRARY OF

THE STORY COLLECTOR

KRISTIN O'DONNELL TUBB

with illustrations by Iacopo Bruno

A New York Public Library Book

SQUARE
FISH

HENRY HOLT & COMPANY · NEW YORK

SQUARE FISH

An imprint of Macmillan Publishing Group, LLC
120 Broadway, New York, NY 10271
mackids.com

Square Fish and the Square Fish logo are trademarks of Macmillan and
are used by Henry Holt and Company under license from Macmillan.

Our books may be purchased in bulk for promotional, educational, or business
use. Please contact your local bookseller or the Macmillan Corporate and
Premium Sales Department at (800) 221-7945 ext. 5442 or by email at
MacmillanSpecialMarkets@macmillan.com.

Library of Congress Cataloging-in-Publication Data
Names: Tubb, Kristin O'Donnell, author. | Bruno, Iacopo, illustrator.
Title: The story collector / Kristin O'Donnell Tubb ;
with illustrations by Iacopo Bruno.
Description: New York : Henry Holt and Company, 2018. |
Summary: A fictional account of eleven-year-old Viviani Joffre Fedeler, who
was born and raised in the New York Public Library, and her older brothers
and best friend Eva, who all try and find out if the library is haunted.
Identifiers: LCCN 2018003709 | ISBN 978-1-250-21144-6 (paperback) |
ISBN 978-1-250-14381-5 (ebook)
Subjects: LCSH: Fedeler, Viviani Joffre—Juvenile fiction. | New York Public
Library—Juvenile fiction. | CYAC: Fedeler, Viviani Joffre—Fiction. |
New York Public Library—Fiction. | Libraries—Fiction. | Haunted
places—Fiction. | Mystery and detective stories.
Classification: LCC PZ7.T796 St 2018 | DDC [Fic]—dc23
LC record available at https://lccn.loc.gov/2018003709

Originally published in the United States by Henry Holt and Company
First Square Fish edition, 2020
Book designed by Rich Deas + Katie Klimowicz
Square Fish logo designed by Filomena Tuosto

1 3 5 7 9 10 8 6 4 2

LEXILE: 740L

For Kathy & Cory, who helped teach me to read using the phone book. I love you, sissies!

CONTENTS

THE
STORY
COLLECTOR

CHAPTER ONE

Baseball,

Dewey Decimal 796.357

SEE ALSO: *sports, World Series*

Some people are story collectors. While others collect seashells, or stuffed animals, or stamps, story collectors wrap themselves in words, surround themselves with sentences, and play with participles, even those pesky, perky dangling ones. They climb over *C*s and mount *M*s and lounge in *L*s. Soon enough they land in the land of homonyms, then, *wham!* They stumble into onomatopoeia, that lovely creaking, booming bit of wordplay—and that, Dear Friend, is where our story begins:

Crack!

The bat swung over Viviani Fedeler's left shoulder, then clattered to the terra-cotta tile floor of the New

York Public Library. She shrieked and ran, red hair flying, nothing short of a firework whizzing about the bases.

"First!" she shouted as her foot landed squarely on the pages of *The Lost Princess of Oz*.

Viviani's older brother John Jr. muttered something unsavory as the ball sailed over his head. John's best pal, Carroll Case, scrambled across the floor, slipping and sliding around the massive carved oak tables until he finally spotted the ball. It was rolling neatly down the aisle between stacks of *Modern Priscilla* magazine and *Whisper*.

As the children of the building superintendent, the Fedelers had played baseball in many rooms of the library, but the Periodical Reading Room was their favorite. It was a perfect square, and if you squinted, the red tile floor looked just like the clay in a baseball diamond.

"Second!" Viviani yelled as she toed *The Bobbsey Twins on Blueberry Island*.

Outside these thick marble walls, a horse-and-buggy trotted alongside clanking trolleys and honking automobiles, over rumbling subways. And on a clear day, if you leaned just right, you could see the gleaming white spire of the Woolworth Building, the tallest building in the world, from this spot at Fifth and Forty-Second.

This room had ample light from multiple windows, and Viviani imagined the trees fluttering in the wind just outside as a stadium full of fans, cheering her on:

Go, Viv! You can do it! She could hear them screaming now: *Head for home, Viviani! Head for home!* She could make it. She *knew* she could make it. She rounded third (a copy of *Once on a Time*) and plowed toward home plate.

Carroll scooped up the ball and hurled it with a grunt. The ball whizzed past Viviani and flew directly at one of the two-story lead-glass windows. A window with frilly woodwork around the sides and thick iron grilles holding the glass in place. An expensive window. One that wouldn't fare well on the wrong end of a speeding baseball.

At the last moment, John Jr. leapt into the air and *thunk!* The ball nestled into his leather glove.

John Jr. touched the base at the exact moment Viviani shouted "HOME!" She slammed into him, and the two toppled over the copy of *The House at Pooh Corner* that served as home plate.

"Out," declared John.

"Am not," said Viviani.

"Are too."

"Am not am not *am not!*"

"Strong argument," Carroll said. "But you are out, Red."

Viviani stuck out her tongue at Carroll and whirled to her teammate and best friend. "Tell them, Eva. Tell them I'm in."

Eva twirled a lock of dark hair about her finger, straightening and releasing a perfect pin curl. "She's in. I'm pretty sure she's in."

Viviani and John Jr. turned to the umpire. "Ump?" said John.

But it was readily apparent that this umpire would be of no use. At least, not where baseball was concerned. The middle Fedeler child, Edouard, sat reading on an overturned garbage can, the ones with the brass lion knockers specially made for the library. His nose was buried deep in first base.

"Fact," Edouard said into the book, which he'd lifted off the baseball diamond as soon as Viviani had toed it. "The national anthem in Oz is 'The Oz Spangled Banner.'"

"Edouard!" Viv and Junior shouted.

"Out," Edouard declared without even bothering to look up.

Viviani cleared her throat and prepared to deliver her protest. She'd start with an appeal to Edouard's finer points: his studiousness, his quiet strength. Then she'd appeal to his vast logical side: she'd explain how it was impossible for John Jr. to have leapt that high, only to

5

have landed at just the right time in just the right place to tag her at home plate. Finally, she'd nail her argument with this: John Jr. must've instead tagged a library goblin, not her. Their father often told stories of the goblins, helpful little creatures that crept around the library stacks at night when all the patrons had gone home. Edouard couldn't resist the one-two punch of a compliment plus a mythical creature.

Then, if all else failed, she would yell at him.

Before Viviani could open her mouth, the children's librarian, Miss Alice Keats O'Conner, entered the room.

With a patron.

"Killjoy," Viviani muttered. Unfortunately, in such a large, high-ceilinged, echoing room, her words were magnified. Viviani cringed. Eva shrank.

"It's not what it looks like," Viviani said weakly.

The keen eyes of Miss O'Conner flew from the panting children to her precious books scattered about the room. A thunderous frown darkened her brow. Her nostrils flared. Her glasses slipped to the tip of her nose, and she crammed them against her eyebrows with a firm finger.

Miss O'Conner puffed up like a balloon. "You were playing baseball. In the Periodical Reading Room."

"Okay, it's exactly what it looks like," Viviani said.

Carroll sputtered a laugh and caught an elbow in the ribs from John Jr.

"You were playing *baseball*?" Miss O'Conner repeated. "In the *Periodical Reading Room*? And oh—you mangled *Pooh!*"

She lifted home base and examined the book in the sunlight glinting through the thank-goodness-she-hadn't-seen-it-nearly-get-smashed window. The book had gotten a tad rumpled. A few pages were bent, and a large, dusty footprint graced the back cover.

"Only improves it, if you ask me," Carroll whispered. "Load of treacle."

This was quite the wrong thing to say, as Pooh held a special place in the hearts of all children's librarians, especially Miss O'Conner's. The librarian considered trampling a book tantamount to trampling the author him- or herself.

"Out!" She stamped her heel—*bam!*—against the tile floor and jabbed a finger at the door. Carroll and John Jr. chuckled and dashed into the hallway. Viviani, who knew Eva's shyness would keep her glued to the spot, grabbed her friend by the wrist and pulled her toward the frosted-glass doors. Miss O'Conner was positively red-faced.

"Your coloring looks really pretty when you get all flustered like that, Miss O'Conner," Viv said as she and

Eva scooted past. "Especially against your pearl earrings." Viv chuckled. "And if you think about it, Miss O'Conner—"

"Viviani Joffre Fedeler," Miss O'Conner said, pushing her glasses up her nose again, "I do not want to hear one of your tales right now."

See, Friend, here's the trouble with having a storyteller's soul: not everyone enjoys a good story all the time. Not even librarians, because sometimes the adult in them overtakes their story-loving side. Too often, people think of stories as fluff or nonsense. Some might even go so far as to call them lies.

"But—" Viviani began.

Miss O'Conner turned redder still and shook her pointer finger. "OUT!"

Edouard never once looked up from *The Lost Princess of Oz*. "Out. That's exactly what I said."

CHAPTER TWO

Games,

Dewey Decimal 790.1

SEE ALSO: *indoor games, activities*

When nightfall weaves its way through the New York Public Library, it is nothing shy of magic. Long stretches of sunlight on marble morph from white to yellow to pink to orange to red, then dim slowly, completely. Shadows yawn and stretch awake. Eighty-five miles of books on shelves blink away their daytime sleep, for books are often nocturnal creatures, ready to play. To roam. To hunt. Or so it seemed to Viviani, who felt as though those stacks of books had eyes.

First, the administrative staff would depart. Viviani would sneak into their offices, just across the main hall from the apartment on the second floor, where her family lived because her father was the building superintendent. Viviani would wheel about in office chairs, and wrap curlicue telephone cords around herself, and bang typewriter keys to the tunes of her favorite songs, such as: *"In the mornin'! In the evenin'! Ain't we got fun!"* (Meanwhile the paper rolled into the typewriter would actually read: *gkrahtiowh! thoshtht! Ahffa ajgkhraso athorah tsghoa!*)

Next, after the librarians straightened the last of the stacks, gathered their belongings, and shut off lamps, they would leave. This was when the fun would *really* start: Viviani would pull books off the shelves to make herself a sizable book fort, with a nice book throne inside. "Off with their heads!" she'd shout, and "Who dares disobey me?" Then she'd stack the books *exactly* back on the shelves in order because as her dad was fond of saying, hell hath no fury like a librarian scorned.

Next, from downstairs came the unmistakable *BOOM!* that signaled the large, ornate iron doors being pulled shut over the main library entrance. The library, which roared like a lion with the sound of eleven thousand visitors passing through its wooden rotating doors each day, fell to a purr and then, finally, to sleep. Once those main doors were closed and locked, the heartbeat of the library quieted, and the building belonged to Viviani and her family.

This particular late-fall evening, Viviani poked her head over the thick marble railing. Two stories below in the lobby, the night guard, jolly old Mr. Eames, jangled his large brass key ring, went to the back of the main entrance hall, and took a left toward the theater while whistling "Yes Sir, That's My Baby."

"I bested you again, sir," Viviani whispered with a smile, and tiptoed down the wide, dark hallway, across the length of the building, and down one flight of stairs. Her destination was the map room, at the far end of the first floor.

But just as Viv was sneaking down the last set of stairs and around the corner, she heard footsteps.

"Ha! Caught you, Red!"

Viviani's heart skipped a beat. She was face-to-face, or rather face-to-finger, with Mr. Eames. Her shoulders fell.

"Five points from your total, missy," Mr. Eames said, pulling a small notebook and pen from his breast pocket. "That leaves you with—"

"Two hundred eighty-five," Viviani and Mr. Eames said in unison. Viviani couldn't help but grin. She stood on tiptoe, trying to see the tally marks scratched in Mr. Eames's notepad. "I'm still in the lead though, right?"

Mr. Eames glanced at the point totals. "No, ma'am. It's been sixteen days since I've seen Edouard. He's the one to beat."

Viviani nodded, cracked her knuckles. "Edouard," she whispered. "Shoulda known." She paused, then added, "Hey, I really like the turkey bow tie. Perfect for Thanksgiving. Gobble, gobble!"

Mr. Eames wore a different bow tie every day, and combined with his sharply creased security guard jacket, he was always quite a spiffy sight. "Flattery will get you nowhere, Viviani," he said, chuckling. "Two hundred eighty-five."

Viviani's lips pursed. "Have you lost weight?"

Mr. Eames laughed, snapped the notebook shut, tucked it back into his pocket, and patted it. "Carry on then, Red." Mr. Eames walked away, whistling and jangling his key ring.

And so the ongoing game of Master Thief continued. Viviani and her brothers could, on most nights, maneuver throughout the library without once seeing Mr. Eames. Not that they didn't care for him: he gave hearty hugs and was quick to share a stick of gum. But each day they managed to avoid him, he awarded them ten points toward their Master Thief status. A "Gotcha!" greeting from Mr. Eames after the library closed set the Fedeler kids back five points.

Viviani entered the moonlight-soaked map room. She adored this room. The walls were painted a soft sky blue; the ceiling, covered in ornate gold carvings. But best of all were the maps. They were everywhere: On the walls. On the shelves. Sprawled open in large atlases across gleaming tabletops. Viviani felt as if she had the whole world at her fingertips when she was in the map room.

She crossed to the sixteenth-century map displayed on the opposite side of the room. It depicted the English Channel and its whereabouts. And the best part: it was covered in sea monsters!

The map always brought to mind Viviani's favorite pirate tale about Lady Mary Killigrew, who dressed like a man and sailed under the name Pyrate Jon-Bonnie. She wished she could be an adventurer like her. Viviani bet that when Lady Mary sailed, the kraken and the sea dragons fled to deep waters because they knew better than to be beheaded by her swift sword.

Oh, how Viviani loved all those stinky old pirates! And oh, how she loved the maps that captured those tales.

Viv sank into a chair and sighed. There were so many exciting stories to collect! Tales of bravery! Tid-bits of tenacity! Fables filled with derring-do! Her life was so boring in comparison. How was she supposed to find her Happily Ever After if she wasn't even sure her Once Upon a Time had started yet?

Viv tugged the fur collar of her overcoat to her cheeks and huffed a cloud of warm breath on her balled fists. Viv and her family often wore coats on chilly evenings in the massive library. While the furnace chugged throughout the night (thanks to Papa's stoking it regularly), the amount of coal used in the evenings was significantly less. She hugged her knees and rocked on the creaky wooden chair.

Viv could go back to their warm library apartment, but she was avoiding home. Her mother, Cornelia Fedeler, would insist she help with cooking dinner. Cooking! Her mother was a real prize at it, and even here, two city blocks north and one floor down, Viviani could smell the heavenly mix of onions and garlic and peppers wafting from their apartment. She pictured the scent as a snake, winding its way through the library until it found her here, in this dark room, tempting her the way Eve was tempted with the apple. *Vivianiiiiiii* . . . , it hissed.

But *cooking*? Where was the danger and excitement in that? One couldn't even gather so much as a skinned knee from cooking. No, she'd simply head back when her mother sounded the dinner gong, chosen and

14

purchased in Chinatown when a bell couldn't be heard throughout this massive building.

Viviani sat, enjoying the quiet and the world on maps all about, until suddenly she felt eyes on her. A shadow passed across the walls. A rustle made the hairs on the back of her neck stand on end. She turned, her chair groaning.

Mr. Green.

Viviani gulped. While everyone knew Mr. Eames's routine, Mr. Green, the library custodian, kept them guessing. No one ever heard him coming.

Mr. Green snuck around the big table at the opposite end of the room. He held a paper trash bag and scooped the leftover scraps of notes and discarded pencil shavings and bent pen nibs into his bag. *Scoop, shuffle, drag.*

Don't be silly, Viviani told herself as she studied Mr. Green's every move. *He's fine. Don't believe what John Jr. says about him.*

Mr. Green's gums smacked.

Viviani shivered. *Just a coincidence*, she thought. *There's nothing to be afraid of.*

Mr. Green worked his jaw back and forth.

Viviani's stomach dropped. *That could be anything.*

Mr. Green blew a slow, pink bubble with the gum in his mouth, and *pop!*

15

"Mr. Green is not a cannibal!"

Unfortunately, yes, Viviani *did* say that aloud. Mr. Green jumped, spilling the contents of the bag he was holding. Refuse went everywhere: a poof of dust and dirt and trash. Mr. Green's brow furrowed. He fixed his glare on Viviani.

Did he just growl? Viviani was sure he growled.

She yelped, leapt up, dashed across the room, through the double leather doors, and up one flight of stairs, slipping and sliding all the way down the hall to the door of her family's apartment. She paused there to catch her breath because her mother could smell mischief a mile away.

John Jr. had once told her that Mr. Green was a cannibal. His words rang through her head now: *That Mr. Green? Oh, you may think he's a custodian, but he would just as soon plop you into that bag of his, Red. Beware!*

Viviani had laughed at the time. "Mr. Green? He's no cannibal."

Junior had narrowed his twinkling eyes at her. "And his custodial closet, the one at the bottom of the basement stairs? The one that's *always locked*?"

"What about it?" Viv had asked, her voice suddenly shaking.

"He's the only one with a key to that closet. No one else has a key like that."

"Yeah, so?"

"*That's* where he hides the evidence. That's where he takes the bones of his victims, Red! That closet of his is a graveyard." John Jr. had cackled wildly, licking his fingertips as if he'd just enjoyed a tasty meal.

"It's not true," Viv had said, shaking to the tips of her toenails.

"Still, it *could* be true, couldn't it?" John Jr. had asked her.

That was a favorite saying of their papa's: It *could* be true. And *could* danced around in Viviani's mind as solidly as *probably*, which was nearly *definitely*. "Just watch where you wander, Red, or else . . . PLOP!" John Jr. had jumped and stamped his foot then, and Viviani and Edouard had yelped.

Viviani was not thick. She knew John Jr. was just teasing her. It was what older brothers did, after all. But once John Jr. said it *could* be true, things became all too real for Viviani Joffre Fedeler.

Viviani's teeth squeaked, she ground them so hard. She gulped a second time. She pushed off the wall and opened the door to head inside the apartment.

Better to help with a cooking pot than to end up inside one!

CHAPTER THREE

Superstitions,

Dewey Decimal 133.43

SEE ALSO: *amulets, charms, talismans*

Story collectors tend to be superstitious. Knock on wood, black cats, four-leaf clovers . . . that sort of thing. After all, superstitions are the little stories we tell ourselves to make sense of our chaotic world.

Every morning, Viviani would hop down the front steps of the library, counting backward as she did, starting at twenty-eight: "Twenty-eight! Twenty-seven! Twenty-six!" until she reached "Three! Two! One!"

Next, she would rub the mane of the lion to the north and bellow, "Good morning, Leo Lenox!" Then she would wave to the lion across the way and holler, "Good morning, Leo Astor!" before running to meet Eva so they could walk to school together.

The reason Viviani did this every morning was simple: two years ago, Viviani performed this morning routine and found a dime while crossing Park Avenue. A whole dime! Granted, this marvelous luck had never repeated itself, but it *could*. And *could* was as good as *definitely*.

This morning's plan was no different. But as Viviani began to hop, she saw that the Doughnut Sisters were back. The Doughnut Sisters! Out on the front steps of the library perched the twins Gladys and Irene McIntyre, all hawkish noses and clawlike fingers. The stodgy duo rang tiny bells and peddled boxes of doughnuts. "Buy a box of doughnuts and—" Gladys shouted.

"—support the Salvation Army!" Irene finished.

"Only one dollar per box to—" Gladys shouted.

"—help the poor and the destitute!" Irene finished.

"You two go fetch your change," John Jr. said as he and Edouard bounded down the steps to join Viviani.

Viviani knew full well that John Jr. was a cheapskate; he could afford to buy three boxes of doughnuts if he wanted. But the only way he'd share was if Edouard and Viv chipped in. After some scrambling, they scraped together ninety-six cents.

Gladys and Irene shook their heads in unison.

"We're only four cents short!" John Jr. pleaded.

"Oh, but it's four cents for the—" Gladys started.

"—poor and destitute, you see." Irene glowered. "Have pity, child."

John Jr.'s lips flattened. He dug deeper into his pocket, where miraculously he found a nickel. "I want that penny change, too."

The twins eyed him with a beady glare and handed over a box of doughnuts and a penny. "Thank you for—"

"—supporting the Salvation Army."

Viviani and Edouard and John Jr. raised their sweet, doughy pastries into a triad. "To your health!" And oh! How light and fluffy and melt-on-your-tongue sugary those doughnuts were. The Doughnut Sisters were vinegar, but their wares were pure honey.

"What a great way to—" Edouard started around a mouthful of dough.

"—start off the day," John Jr. interrupted. And they all laughed.

Except.

Except Viviani forgot all about her superstitions.

Perhaps her lack of rituals might have been *exactly* why things changed so drastically that day.

Licking her fingers, Viviani crossed Fifth Avenue, then pulled on her mittens. She met Eva at the corner. Together, they walked to school, mitten in soggy mitten, over Madison, Park, and Lexington, past the Hotel Belmont ("Good day, George!" Viviani shouted to the doorman, who saluted in return), under the rumbling elevated train tracks on Third, until they reached Public School 27. It was a fine and sturdy redbrick school building with a grand edifice, but lacking in the elegance of front-stoop lionry, which in Viviani's opinion every stoop should offer.

Viviani fidgeted throughout her morning classes: Latin (yawn), math (yay!), and needlework (yuck). While Viv knotted colorful threads into a tapestry of a fox outwitting some hounds, Eva crocheted. Or attempted to.

"I'm . . . getting better, don't you think, Viv?" She held up her blanket and peered through one of the many wide holes in her creation.

"You are, Eva," Viviani said encouragingly.

Eva scrutinized her handiwork. "I am getting better . . . better at making fishing nets."

The girls exploded with laughter until Miss Hutch shushed them with a single arched eyebrow.

The classroom door creaked open, and a girl with sleek, dark hair and wide, nervous eyes peered in.

"Class!" Miss Hutch quieted them with a loud handclap. "We have a new student joining us today. Merit, come in, come in! Tell us about yourself."

Merit glided to the front of the room, eyes lowered,

and it was easy to see she had the heebie-jeebies. Viviani had been in this same boring old school building her whole life and thought it must have been hard to start at a new school. When Merit tucked a strand of her long (not pinned-up!) hair behind her ear, Viviani saw that she wore shiny gold hoop earrings. Viv sat up straighter. Anyone with pierced ears was probably worth listening to.

"I'm Merit. Merit Mubarak. My family just moved here from Giza, Egypt."

Merit's accent was melodic, crisply chopped, like a British accent. Viviani decided in that instant that Merit would be a fine third musketeer to her and Eva.

"Tell us a little about Giza, Merit," Miss Hutch said.

Merit toed the linoleum with her very fashionable shoe, and the shiny gold buckle on it gleamed. These weren't your everyday Mary Janes. Merit was not your everyday Mary Jane.

"Well," Merit said slowly, "it's very hot. And dry. And flat. But there are lots of palm trees and fun things to do, like climb the pyramids."

"You can climb the pyramids?" Jake Joseph shouted. He sounded impressed. And Viviani knew firsthand that Jake Joseph was hard to impress.

"Raise your hand, please," Miss Hutch reminded the class.

"You can climb the pyramids?!" Jake Joseph shouted again as his hand shot skyward. "How tall are they?"

Merit's eyes lit up as she thought of her home. "Tall. About like a four-story building here. I've never made it to the top, but my father has."

"Wow!"

"Nifty!"

"That is the bee's knees!"

Viviani couldn't remember the last time she'd said something about herself that was the bee's knees.

Merit's chin lifted a little more. "And my family had two camels. They were mainly to carry things. We didn't ride them very often."

"You've ridden a camel?" Viviani shouted. When she saw Miss Hutch scowl at her, she raised her hand while waiting for Merit to answer.

Merit laughed. "Yes. It's not much different from riding a horse."

Viviani's cheeks felt hot. She'd never even ridden a horse. *Behind* a horse, in a carriage, sure. Fake ones on a carousel, sure. But she'd rarely left the eight-block radius around the library. As big as her home was, it didn't have real, live pyramids and camels and gold earrings. Did she even have a single story of her own worth sharing?

Merit's adventures were what real stories were made

of. At that moment, Viviani determined to wedge herself inside Merit's tale, too. Surely then, her story would be as exciting and adventurous as a true storybook character's.

This was where her Once Upon a Time would start.

CHAPTER FOUR

Inventions,

Dewey Decimal 609.2

SEE ALSO: *inventors, technological innovations*

"Twelve gulps! Beat that, Eva!" Viviani had just proved she could slug from the lion-headed water fountain twelve whole times before her belly began to slosh. Viviani stepped aside and shook out the front of her soaked dress. Eva approached the water fountain and jogged in place, like a prizefighter in training. Viviani laughed. Until Eva undertook the challenge: twenty-one gulps!

"Wow!" Viviani said, clapping her friend on the back. "Twenty-one! You're swimming from the inside out, Eva!"

Eva panted and nodded and swiped her dress sleeve across her mouth.

It was Saturday at last, which was the niftiest and slowest-arriving and fastest-passing day of the week. Viviani and Eva had already raced the elevators up and down the top three floors, spied on the lecture about life on Mars that was taking place in the first-floor auditorium, and climbed and leapt off the bases of the ornately carved flagpoles outside. Yesterday, Viviani had asked Merit to join them, but she shook her head, saying she needed to go to the market with her uncle to translate for him. Viviani felt a bit jealous when she learned that Merit spoke two languages. Imagine how many stories you could collect with double the words!

"I'm bored," Viviani declared almost immediately. "Let's go invent something."

Viviani was rather determined to make good on her promise to live a more exciting and adventurous life. She thought of her literary heroes. Robert from *Five Children and It*. Sahwah from the Camp Fire Girls. Alice and Dora Bastable from *The Wouldbegoods*. They were always inventing and exploring and adventuring.

"Invent? Where?" Eva asked.

"My papa's workshop," Viviani said.

"The workshop?"

"The workshop."

Eva chewed on her bottom lip. "I thought you weren't allowed in your papa's workshop."

"That was when I was younger." Viviani shrugged. "He hasn't said not to go in there in at least six months."

Eva shot Viviani a bit of the old side-eye, but Viviani was already tugging her toward the stairs. Viviani was always tugging Eva somewhere.

The basement—at least the part where the workshop was located—was far from cheery. But Viviani knew that sometimes one must face unpleasant things for the sake of conquering crushing boredom.

The two girls tiptoed down the solid stairs, hands knotted. They crept slowly up to a heavy metal door, which Viviani heaved open with a grunt. This part of the basement was cold and dark, with a lonely dripping sound echoing off the stone walls—*drip, drip, drip*—and the sound brought to Viviani's mind the idea of pooling blood. She shook that thought off—she'd recently read Edgar Allan Poe's "The Tell-Tale Heart." Miss O'Conner had forbidden her from reading it, saying it was much too scary for little girls, which naturally meant Viviani couldn't resist devouring the blood-curdling tale in one sitting. Oh, that terrifying heart! Viviani swore she could *hear* it thumping as she'd read the story. (Or perhaps it had been her own racing pulse?) Now every sound in the library made Viviani jump.

The basement was, in fact, the site of an old city reservoir, and the walls were from the old basin. They had a cave-like look to them, worn by years of holding water prior to their years of bolstering books. Viviani felt like a spelunker on a cave exploration the few times she'd been in this section of the building, and she often thought she might see stalactites and stalagmites and hordes of bats. And bat guano.

She and Eva crept between the chiseled rock walls, under the low-hanging, pipe-strewn ceiling. They tiptoed down a long, narrow hallway, lined on both sides with tables, chairs, molding—all broken, all needing her papa's attention.

Viviani and Eva continued making their way to the workshop, passing the fiery boiler room through a hissing blast of dry heat. It had the distinct chalky smell of coal, and the air felt gritty and particularly full of darkness in this spot. It was the coal dust, Viviani knew, but it felt like walking through a grimy shadow.

In a dark nook at the bottom of the basement stairs stood the one place in the whole library where Viviani had *never* been: the custodian's closet. The one that belonged to Mr. Green, the one that was always locked tight. Always. Viviani's blood ran cold, thinking of what John Jr. had told her, thinking of what might be locked away behind that thick iron door. Nests of snakes? Vials of poison? *Bones from his victims?*

"Viviani."

The two girls squeaked and turned toward the voice: Miss O'Conner. The children's area was also in the basement, but in a far cheerier spot, with yellow-painted walls and an outside door and sunlight. Here, in the shadows-and-coal portion of the basement, Miss O'Conner loomed over them like a giantess.

Her glasses slipped to the tip of her nose, and she crammed them back up the bridge with a knobby knuckle. "We are missing several picture books from the children's section of the library," she said. "Would you and your . . . *fellow baseball players*"—here she glared at Eva, who gulped—"know anything about that?"

"Picture books? I haven't read picture books in years."

Miss O'Conner scoffed, which caused her glasses to slip again. "One is never too old for picture books, Viviani."

Viviani huffed. Just because she enjoyed a game of baseball with her brothers didn't mean she was a thief. "I don't know anything about the missing picture books, Miss O'Conner. Sorry."

Miss O'Conner shoved her glasses to the top of her head, into her nest of hair. "I should hope not, but of course I had to check. Good day." She turned smartly on her heel and *clackclackclack*ed away, back toward the hallway lined with staff lockers.

Nearby, pistons hummed and one popped, making both girls jump. The churning pistons powered elevators and lights and a small, jazzy radio in the Fedeler apartment overhead, so Viviani was grateful for them, even though they sounded like a racing heartbeat. A spiderweb of wires and pipes hung overhead, pointing the way to her papa's workshop.

Inside the workshop, all sorts of inventions in various states of assembly crowded the tables. Tools, metal bits, electrical wire, Bakelite, fan blades—all of them teetered in haphazard piles about the room.

Papa's workshop was the home of his many tinkerings; he was a man with as many ideas for inventions as there were stars in the sky, or so Viviani thought. But the difficult part in having that many shiny things to tinker with: it was difficult to pick just one. Papa fiddled with everything from indoor cooling units to blowtorches, and they all lived beside one another in his cluttered space.

The workshop was a dimly lit, low-ceilinged room with tools and pliers and shards of metallic things strewn about. Eva toed a saw blade. "This place looks like a dungeon."

"It is," Viviani whispered. "It's where Miss O'Conner puts children who are late with library book returns."

Eva giggled despite herself.

Viviani loved that her best friend was always so ready with a laugh. Eva and her family lived in the Rogers Peet department store across from the library on Forty-Second. When she moved in across the street, Eva and Viv became friends "as fast as a pigeon can poop," Viv would always say. Eva and Viviani would play Hollywood starlet and dress up in the fancy clothes at the department store until Eva's dad scolded them in Armenian.

"Are we even allowed in here?" Eva asked, her eyes scanning the sharp things, the pointy things, the things that slice.

"Of course!" Viv said, though Viv said *of course* to a lot of things that most likely did not fall into the *of course* category. "But first, we need to hang a sign for our Inventors' Club."

Eva grinned. "Inventors' Club?"

"Yep."

Viviani scrawled a quick sign on a yellowing piece of paper torn from a crumbling book, one that the binding department down the hall had decided was beyond repair. Old book pages were what all the library folks used for scrap paper. One supposes there are worse ways for a book to perish than to end up carrying one final message:

INVENTORS' CLUB!

Stay away if you are:

—John Jr. or Edouard

—Unimaginative

—Not Inventive

Viviani chewed on the tip of her pencil, thinking of the locked closet at the end of this very hallway. She hastily added:

—Cannibals!

Then Viv realized that likely wasn't specific enough, because while she did indeed wish to keep out cannibals, she wanted to fend off one in particular. Miss Hutch was always telling them to *be specific* in their writing. So she struck through that and wrote:

—Cannibals! *Mr. Green*

Viviani tacked the note to the door, then picked up a small telegraph machine whose wiry guts spilled through its removed back side. "Let's invent something to talk to Martians!"

Eva found a few small, valuable knobs of tinfoil, and they fashioned a bowl out of it, connecting wires and clamps all around. Soon, their creation looked like a rather proper tool for communicating with Mars.

"Let's see if we get a signal!" Viviani stretched and stretched and stretched, but the cord didn't quite make it to the plug box. After some table shifting and heavy lifting, they plugged in their invention with great anticipation, and . . .

"Nothing," Viv said, blowing on the exposed copper wire ends and jiggling the contraption. "Rats." She looked up at Eva. "Looks like we won't get to chat with any Martians today."

Eva's eyes were wide. She lifted her chin toward the doorway. Before Viviani even turned to see what might be there, a chill raced over her skin. She felt eyes on her, like she was being watched.

A murky, disheveled figure stood in the shadows of the hallway. Something about the way the shadow moved seemed unnatural—silent and floating, rather than solid. Even as it got closer, Viviani couldn't hear any footsteps.

Another piston popped down the hall, and Eva let out a little shriek.

Eva clutched Viviani's hand. Her grip was cold and clammy. The best friends watched as the shadow slipped away without a word.

Viviani took a deep, quivery breath. "Let's go."

CHAPTER FIVE

Ghosts,

Dewey Decimal 133.1

SEE ALSO: *spirits, hauntings, apparitions*

Viviani and Eva took off from the workshop at a full
sprint, the soles of their shoes sliding and slipping
and squeaking on the basement floor. They rounded
the corner and pounded up a half flight of stairs.

"Girls!"

Viviani ran—*oof*—right into Papa's chest. Papa!

Her racing heart leapt into her throat. She and Eva
placed hands on knees, panting.

"Where were you two?" Papa asked, his eyes narrow
but shining.

Viviani swallowed. "Uh . . . Miss O'Conner. She's
looking for lost picture books."

It wasn't a lie, and so Eva, always-honest Eva, nodded.

Papa's eyes slid between the two of them. "Missing picture books? That's the emergency?"

Viviani gulped for air. "There are lost stories out there, Papa. Wouldn't you call that an emergency?"

Papa stroked his jaw. "Hmmm. Carry on then." He waved them up the last half flight of stairs.

When the two friends reached the first floor, Viviani stopped for a moment and placed her cheek against the cool wall to steady herself. Maybe it was the twelve gulps of water, or maybe it was the custodial closet, or maybe it was that strange, floating figure near the workshop, or maybe it was the fact that she knew she shouldn't have been in the workshop in the first place, but Viviani felt downright ill.

She wouldn't get in trouble, though. She'd covered her tracks with Papa.

Boy, living a life of excitement and adventure sure was full of turmoil!

The next day, Viviani's papa returned to their apartment following his rounds covered in sawdust and coal dust and dust-dust. He sat at the dinner table. "Today I was a furniture fixer, and a wheel replacer for a book cart, and a radio-antenna repairman, and an untangler of telephone wire." Viviani thought his might be the best job on earth: fixing things meant every day was different from the last.

Viv plopped into her place at the dinner table and scowled. "Liver and onions?"

Oops. Once again, Viviani's mouth was too fast for her brain. And this time, her words were coated in disgust because, well, *liver and onions*.

Mama arched a teasing eyebrow at Viv. "If you help make dinner, Red, you get a say in what gets served."

"Fact," Edouard said around a mouthful. "Your liver functions as a filter for toxins. Without it, you'd slowly poison yourself." He swallowed.

All eyes turned to Edouard. He paused, the next forkful of quivering liver halfway to his mouth. "What?"

"Here's a fact for ya," John Jr. said, buttering a slice of bread. "Babe Ruth is the greatest baseball player of all time."

"That's not fact. That's opinion."

"Yeah, well, his sixty home runs last year prove it. There should be a display about him at the library."

Mama nodded. "I like that idea, John. Talk to Dr. Anderson and see what he thinks. He'd be the one to approve the funding and rally the librarians. I'd personally love to see a display on jazz. The radio station here could play a little of the Boswell Sisters? Maybe some Jelly Roll Morton?" Mama hummed a few bars and danced a tiny jig while plopping mashed potatoes on everyone's plate.

Papa smiled and tapped his toe to the rhythm. "That's my love! Always shaking things up."

"I'd like to see one on airships," Edouard said, swallowing a mouthful of potatoes. "Fact: Henri Giffard was actually the first person to fly. In 1852, he flew seventeen miles in a dirigible."

Papa gulped down a glass of milk, then poured another. "How about you, Red? What kind of display would you like to see?"

Viviani's head spun. She didn't know what she wanted to know. No, that wasn't it; she wanted to know *so much*. How radios and telegraphs work and how subways are built and why kittens are born with their eyes closed and how to speak Greek and all about feathers and shells and weather. Everyone else in her family seemed to know exactly what interested them. *Everything* interested Viviani.

"I can't pick just one," Viv said. "I want to know it all."

Papa tossed his head back and laughed.

John Jr. said, "Good news. I think you're already a know-it-all," and lightly punched her arm. Viviani laughed and pretended to fling back a spoonful of liver.

But the conversation niggled at the back of her mind: How come everyone else knew exactly what they wanted to know and say? And how come she didn't?

After dinner, Papa settled into his great armchair with his slippers and a mug of coffee.

"Kids!" he called out. Papa's large, lanky frame far exceeded what was likely considered comfortable for the size of his armchair, but it was his favorite nonetheless.

Viviani and her siblings scrambled to gather around Papa's chair. It was story time!

Edouard snagged the patch of carpet just in front of Papa. "Papa! Tell us a story of when you worked for Thomas Edison."

"Who cares about some boring inventor?" John Jr. whacked Edouard with a needlepoint pillow. "What a wet blanket. Let's hear one of your sailing tales, Papa!"

Viviani slid down the walnut-paneled wall. "I want to hear the story of how I was given my name! That's my favorite." Viv's brothers groaned.

"No, no, kids," Papa waved off their suggestions. "Tonight, I want to tell you about the Red-Whiskered Ghost."

"Yes!" Edouard hugged the pillow that had whacked him.

John Jr. rolled his eyes, but Viviani grabbed a pillow

to clutch as well. *Ghost?* Instantly, she thought of the shadowy figure she had seen near Papa's workshop.

"This library, these walls!" Papa boomed, swooping his arms wide across their wood-paneled apartment. "They took a decade to build, you know. And over the course of those ten long years, ten men unfortunately lost their lives. Ten men!"

At that precise moment, Mama turned off the electric light from the kitchen. The sudden darkness caused a collective gasp from the Fedeler children. Mama chuckled. She loved Papa's stories as much as her kids did.

Papa took a sip of his coffee. "To this day, the spirits of those fallen men wander these very halls, demanding to know: Is the vast knowledge contained within these walls *worth their very lives*?"

"Of course it is," Edouard said. "Knowledge is a noble cause!"

Papa winked at his middle child. "But the angriest ghost of the whole gang is an old red-whiskered fellow."

"Of course he has a beard," John Jr. said with a chuckle. "How would a ghost shave?"

Papa winked at his eldest child as well. A two-winker tale, this one was. "This particular apparition," he continued, "was a red-haired, red-whiskered bulk of a man, whose job it was to hang the ornate plaster on the ceiling of the Main Reading Room."

Viviani pictured the famous room: the carved plaster ceiling looked like it was covered in curly icicles. Ornate borders painted to look like wood framed a mural of blue skies and sunshine-rimmed clouds. Massive bronze chandeliers, each with dozens of glowing globes of light, plunged from the great height. The ceiling was several stories high, hovering far, far above the marble floors below. Viviani shuddered, thinking of those workers clinging to flimsy metal scaffolding, lying on their backs and hoisting those heavy chunks of plaster overhead while hammering them into place.

"Yes indeedy, it was this fella's job to secure those carvings with large, long spikes. He was good at it, too. The best, according to him. He'd brag and he'd boast and he'd drive his coworkers to distraction with it all. One day, he waged a bet against another worker that he'd finish the ceiling before that worker finished tiling a floor. Faster and faster he worked, securing those plaster carvings.

"But one day, after hammering home the next-to-last spike on the very last carving, this guy rose up in a celebratory yalp. He was just about to win that bet, you see—a whole month's salary, and he wanted everyone to see him drive home the last nail. But instead, the old fella lost his balance and fell off the scaffolding to his untimely death."

The Fedeler kids sat in silence, for this was the protocol after stories of untimely death.

"It was his own boastfulness that did that fella in. He never got to pocket that money, and he never got to finish that ceiling. And so you should know: the Red-Whiskered Ghost still wanders these very halls, hammer in hand. He was gambling and showboating, you see. Killed by his own mischief. And now he seeks to destroy mischief whenever it is near."

Goose bumps arose on Viviani's skin. She thought back to the figure she and Eva had seen in the workshop, where, all right, perhaps a *little* bit of mischief was involved. Had she heard a clanging sound? One like a hammer might make? She covered her arms before anyone saw and teased her for being a scaredy-cat.

"So, kids"—Papa's eyes narrowed but twinkled, and his voice dropped to a teasing whisper—"no hijinks, or—"

WHAM! Papa stamped his foot, and all three Fedeler kids jumped. But only two laughed.

Could everyone hear Viviani's heart thrumming? Surely they could. Just like in "The Tell-Tale Heart."

Edouard shivered with the deliciousness of the tale. "What was his name? The guy?"

Papa downed the rest of his coffee. "His name? Why, you know what they call our library ghost?"

The Fedeler kids shook their heads.

"They call him . . . *Big Red*!" Papa's eyes widened. Viviani's fingers flew to her flaming hair.

"Hey, just like your nickname, Viv!" Edouard grinned.

"Big Red! And you're Little Red! Like me and Papa— John Junior and Senior. Ha!" John Jr. reached over to tug a lock of her hair.

Viviani did not like that, no sir. She didn't care for that one bit.

"There is no ghost, and he is most certainly not named Red." She shook her head. She *harrumph*ed. She crossed her arms. "It's not true." Sometimes stating things aloud was the way to convince yourself to believe it.

Papa ruffled his daughter's fiery curls. "Ah, but watch where you go and what you do in this place! Big Red seeks out mischief, and he could be out there with his hammer *right now*!"

Viviani gulped, as if she were swallowing the story whole. Because as all story collectors know, *could* was as good as *probably*, and *probably* was as good as *definitely*.

"So what you're saying is," John Jr. said, rising off the floor, "stop messing around in the off-limits spots in the library."

Papa chuckled, then gave Viviani a long, thoughtful look.

Viviani squeezed the pillow tighter. She didn't want to admit to being a tiny bit petrified. Her brothers seemed both unaffected and unastounded at finding out their home was haunted. She guessed one must be at least twelve years old to be so brave in the face of a grim ghost tale. In that case, she'd look forward to being brave next year.

Viviani decided she needed to talk to Eva and get her thoughts on this ghostly matter. Eva was as reliable as the five-fifteen commuter ferry out of the city, as steady and concrete as the Brooklyn Bridge. If anyone could help Viviani turn this *could* into an *impossible*, it would be Eva.

CHAPTER SIX

Biographies,

Dewey Decimal 937.09

SEE ALSO: *women—biographies; American history—biographies*

*S*creeeee!

The sound woke Viviani from a thin and restless sleep. She bolted upright at the sound just outside her window, clutching her sheet beneath her chin. It sounded like the hooked edge of a hammer clawing across the glass: *screeeeeee!*

Viviani *screeeeeee*d as well.

The radiator banged to life, and she whimpered.

"Viviani?" Mama rushed into her room, tying her robe around her waist. "Is everything all right?"

Papa ran in after her, wielding a baseball bat, eyes wide. When Viviani saw him, her own eyes filled with tears.

She pointed at her dark window. "I thought I heard something out there!"

Mama flicked on the light and crossed to look out the glass. The late-autumn wind stirred, and a tree in the adjacent courtyard reached toward Viviani's window and scratched the glass: *screeeeeee.*

Viviani choked on a sob. "It's okay, Mama, Papa. I just . . . got scared, is all."

Mama cleared her throat and shot Papa a look. Papa sighed and laid the bat next to her bed with a *clunk.* "About Big Red?"

Viviani looked at her quilt and nodded. It swam underneath her gaze.

Mama rubbed her back.

"That's a story, Viviani." Papa's voice was gentle but firm. "I didn't mean to scare you, and I'm sorry I did. But I'm certain you're familiar with mischief. You *cannot* play in the workshop. Understand?"

A tear toppled over the rim of her eye at last.

He knew? How? She thought he'd been too busy with library business to tinker in his workshop lately.

Viviani nodded and took a deep, wavery breath. It was meant to hold back more tears. It didn't work.

Papa rubbed the stubble on his jaw and began:

"The month was May, the year 1917, and at the entrance to the library, the lions Leo Astor and Leo

Lenox wore wreaths of lilies and roses to welcome visiting dignitaries from France. The United States had just entered the Great War, you see, and France was our friend. Inside, a glittering celebration with rich food and bubbly drinks took place on the third floor. On the second floor, a child born only two days prior wailed. I mean, really *wailed*. She had flaming-red hair and an impressive set of lungs, that one. But what she didn't have was a name."

Mama smiled and smoothed her daughter's red hair. Viviani let out a small sob and laughed at the same time.

"The fact that the child had no name troubled her father greatly." Here, Papa pointed to himself. "Oh, how my shoes clacked as I paced the wide marble floors of the library."

Papa leapt up and began acting out the story, the story that had taken place in this very library eleven years prior. He continued:

"'No name!' I said," Papa muttered to himself, scratching his head. "'No name! Why, a child might as well not have a head as have no name.'"

Viviani was laughing deeply now. This was her favorite story of all.

"'Naming sons is pie!' I said to Mr. Green." Papa

must've seen Viviani flinch at the mention of Mr. Green's name, for he added: "Ah, but we cannot forget Mr. Green, you see. If it weren't for him, the rest of the story would not follow, and you'd likely still be nameless."

Mama chuckled and Papa continued: "I said to him, 'Why, it was easy enough to name my firstborn: John Junior—no imagination needed there! And number two, Edouard. Named for my best friend, a sailor like none other. Done and done!'

"At that, Mr. Green, as always, grunted." Papa pointed at Viviani now, who played her part by grunting with gusto.

Papa smiled and began pacing again, the conundrum of his nameless daughter written on his face.

"But a *girl*! I had no idea what to name a girl!

"I had taken to calling you Red, of course—that glorious head of hair. But Red isn't a *name*. And this wasn't just any girl—it was a girl born in this very library! Between the stacks! Among the pages of the finest words ever written! I knew a name for a child like that required brilliance!"

Papa jabbed a finger skyward. Viviani laughed and blushed as red as her hair.

"The sound of tinkling glasses and delicate laughter drifted down the wide hallway from the Main

Reading Room." Papa cocked his ear toward the world-renowned room now, and Viviani could *almost* hear the festivities.

"It was then I realized I was spinning an electric lightbulb in my hand. My errand of changing out a bulb had been forgotten.

"'A name can wait, I suppose,' I declared. 'But that dimmed lamp cannot. Let there be lamplight!' And so I climbed to the top of a tall ladder, all the while muttering, 'a name, a name.'"

"And then the railroad man appeared!" Viviani burst out.

"Yes, that's right. The railroad tycoon James Stillman strutted into the hallway with two guests of honor trailing behind."

Viviani closed her eyes and imagined the dapper trio with their gleaming brass buttons marching up each chest, bow ties blossoming at their throats, and their hair slicked into place with thick, fruity-smelling pomade.

"Mr. Stillman, being an astute businessman and therefore a reader of people, noticed the distraught look on my face.

"'What's wrong, sir?' he asked.

"I spun and teetered on the ladder." Here, Papa pretended to falter, arms and legs flailing, and Viviani and Mama giggled. "'Ah, it's nothing, sir!' I said, for I know better than to muddle in library affairs. 'Thank you for asking. Enjoy your event.'

"Mr. Stillman narrowed his gaze on me, his thin mustache twitching.

"That's the moment Mr. Green coughed up my troubles. 'Aye, it's his newborn, sir. The child is two days old, and still it doesn't have a name.'

"Stillman chuckled, and his eyes glinted as bright as the gold watch chain that draped across his chest. 'If it's a girl,' he told me, 'name her Viviani after this fine Frenchman here.' He slapped his hand on the shoulder of the gentleman to his right. That man was René Viviani, the former prime minister of France. Mr. Viviani guffawed, and his big belly heaved." Papa gave a belly-busting laugh and puffed out his stomach.

"'And if it's a boy, why, you can name him Joffre, after the honorable marshal.' Mr. Stillman winked at the gentleman on his left.

"Stillman grabbed a wreath and handed it to me. 'Congratulations, sir,' he said. And with that, the three illustrious men were on their way.

"Meanwhile, there I was: still teetering atop my tall perch, a wreath in one hand, scratching my head with the other, all while still gripping that silly lightbulb. Can you picture it? That when the very idea of your name sank into my head, the lightbulb was in a quite symbolic spot."

Viviani giggled, imagining the bulb illuminating above her papa's head—*click!*

"And then a baby's wail wafted from below." Here, Papa craned his ear as if toward this very apartment, and Viviani imagined a baby's cries filling the cavernous library. *Her* cries.

" 'A powerful set of lungs needs a powerful set of names,' I said, to which Mr. Green grunted. I leapt off the ladder and flew down the stairs.

" 'Cornelia!' I bounded into the apartment, leaving a trail of flower petals in my wake. Mama was snuggled in bed, nursing our young daughter."

Here, Mama fluffed Viviani's pillow, and Viviani snuggled into her own bed.

" 'My dear Cornelia. We have a name.' " Papa knelt by the bed, flourishing an imaginary wreath.

" 'We do?' " Mama chimed in with her part. Papa's face lit up—very little pleased him as much as when his family indulged his stories.

" 'We do!' I shouted. Then I lifted you up and declared, 'I present to you: Viviani Joffre Fedeler!' "

Here, Papa scooped Viviani up and hoisted her in the air, grunting with the effort. Viviani squirmed and laughed.

"And you did what any hungry, cold baby would do: you let out a blood-curdling yalp."

Viviani glanced at her mother, to see if she could yalp now. Her mother raised her *I believe you know the answer to that, young lady* eyebrow, so Viviani simply pretended to yalp with a small squeak.

Papa gently lowered Viviani into bed and tucked the blankets over her.

"That powerful cry of yours echoed and absorbed into the thousands of books lining the shelves. And in return, those books awakened, unfurling their words, their worlds, slowly, quietly, until stories became as much a part of you as your red hair, your green eyes."

Mama hugged Viviani to her side and kissed the top of her head. Viviani's heart swelled.

"Do you think you can sleep now?" Papa asked.

She nodded. And she meant it.

Mama and Papa left, clicking off the light behind them. Viviani breathed deeply and curled further into her quilt.

Hearing her favorite story had calmed her. It had made her braver. Familiar stories do that. They're as much a part of our identity as the backs of our hands. If we were zebras, our stories would be our stripes. If we were pilots, they would be our compass. If we were adventurers, they'd be our North Star. Our stories are what make us unique. The combination of stories in our lives—the unique mix of the stories we choose to read, choose to live—makes each of us just a tiny bit different from everyone else on the planet. Viviani knew that we are our stories.

At last, Viviani was able to drift into a deep sleep.

Well, also, Papa had left the bat.

CHAPTER SEVEN

Storytelling Techniques,
Dewey Decimal 372.64

SEE ALSO: *storytelling, United States; storytelling, juvenile literature*

Three things happened to Viviani before she even left the library the following morning, and as any good storyteller knows, everything happens in threes:

Number one: Viviani had just woken up and was adding to her wallpaper mural. The walls of her room were covered with yellow-flowered paper that, if stared at long enough, began to take on familiar shapes, like leopards and dragons and an entire family of mice at a picnic. Mama didn't much care for it when Viviani used an ink pen to add whiskers and spots and fiery breath, so she took care to embellish only the sliver of space between her bed and the wall.

"Viv!"

Viviani's skeleton nearly jumped straight out of her skin. Her pen clattered to the floor. "John Junior! Why would you scare me like that?"

"'Cause you always fall for it?" Junior laughed and flopped onto her bed. He jerked his head toward the door. "What'd you do?"

"What do you mean, What did I do?"

"There was a reason Papa told us that story last night. Edouard says it wasn't him, so you had to have done something."

Viviani bit her lip. "Eva and I played in Papa's workshop."

Junior whistled long and low. "Even *I* wouldn't pull that stunt, Red."

Viviani rubbed her tired eyes. "I know. That stupid ghost story kept me up half the night until Papa came in and told me it wasn't true."

John Jr. bolted upright, eyes wide. "Oh, that story is true."

Viviani's heart fluttered. "No, it's not. Papa said he told us that story to keep us out of the workshop."

John Jr. shook his head. "Maybe he did, but it's still true. I've heard the librarians talk about the library ghost. Miss O'Conner says her stuff moves around all the time, and once her glasses even fogged over *in the middle of the library*. Even Dr. Anderson says lights turn on and off unexplainably. It's true."

Viviani gulped. Dr. Anderson? No way. He was the *library director*, for heaven's sake! "I don't believe you."

John Jr. shrugged and rolled off her bed. "You don't have to believe me. You just have to believe what you see. Or *don't* see. WOOOOoooooooOOOO!"

John Jr. backed out of her room, making ghost noises and waving his fingers about until Viviani threw her pillow at him.

Number two: at breakfast, Mama placed a hard-boiled egg on each plate.

"John Junior, Edouard." The radio in the corner kicked out a spicy jazz tune, and the host talked about the perfect fall weather.

"Viviani."

Viv sat up in her chair, because that *Viviani* had a sit-up-straight tone to it. "If this is about that stray cat, Mama, you need to ask John Junior about it."

John Jr.'s lips pulled into a flat line.

"This isn't about a—what? There's not a cat in this library, is there? Junior?"

"No, ma'am. Of course not."

Mama sighed and sank into her chair. "Never mind. I'll deal with that later. Viviani, what in the world were you doing in that workshop?"

Viviani gulped. "Inventing things?"

Mama shook her head in the way that only mamas can to make you feel so, so sorry.

"Viviani, we've discussed this. Anywhere *but* the workshop. There are too many dangerous things in that part of the basement, and I don't want to see you or Eva hurt." Viv's mother tucked a strand of hair behind Viviani's ear, and it felt directly connected to her heart.

"We've asked you not to go into that room many times," her mother continued. "So for the next two weeks, come right back here after school for chores."

Viviani's throat swelled. Two weeks of extra chores! And right before the upcoming winter break from school—how positively awful!

"Red, we trust you. You're a peach of a kid. But you didn't just stretch a truth here, my love. You chose to ignore a rule. That's dangerous." Her mother kissed her forehead.

"I'm sorry, Mama. I got carried away." Viviani's eyes stung.

"Yes," her mother said with a smile. "My Viviani gets carried away so often, she's likely to wind up on the far side of the moon."

Number three: Viviani was just about to push through the rotating front door on her way to school when a grunt from behind made her jump.

"Hey. Kid."

She turned, and there she stood, face-to-face with Mr. Green!

Did he lick his lips? No, she imagined that. Most certainly. But for a moment, Viviani thought what a good story it would make if he did try to gobble her up.

He pressed something into Viviani's hand. "You forgot this the other day." Before she could reply, he slid away, his shoes as silent as blades on ice.

Viviani unclenched her fist. It was a folded sheet of paper. She smoothed it open.

It was the sign Viv made earlier. The INVENTORS' CLUB sign.

Viviani's heart leapt into her throat. He saw that she'd called him a cannibal. She turned the sign over in her hand.

It all made sense. *He'd* ratted her out. He'd gotten angry about the sign, and he'd shown it to Mama and Papa. He'd told them she had been playing in the workshop. Tattletale!

Viviani's cheeks burned. She crammed the sign into her jacket pocket. It was one thing to have your brothers rat on you, but Mr. Green? What business was it of his? Just because they shared the same building didn't mean she had to like him. Not one bit.

So you see, Dear Friend, these three things combined to make Viviani's stomach feel like a fizzy, gurgling Coca-Cola poured straight from a soda fountain.

She felt green and sick. When Merit Mubarak said "Hello, Viviani!" for the first time ever walking into school that morning, Viviani simply nodded and kept walking.

Had that greeting happened any other day than this one, Merit's hello would've made Viviani's heart sing. But instead, Viviani sank into a chair, and Eva answered Merit's cheery hello. Viviani watched the next plot twist unfold, as Eva said something that made Merit toss her head back with laughter, and the two hung their coats next to each other. Viviani thought she could not feel lower.

She was wrong.

CHAPTER EIGHT

Stamp Collecting,
Dewey Decimal 769.56

SEE ALSO: *postage stamps, collectors & collecting*

Just as Viviani was turning the knob to head inside her family's apartment that afternoon, a strong hand clamped her shoulder.

Viviani spun, fists clenched and raised, fight ready, because even though her brain had pushed aside ghosts and groundings and cannibals, her heart hadn't. Hearts can do that, you know: hold on to something when the rest of you has forgotten about it. Hearts have longer memories than brains.

Papa laughed. "Methinks thou dost imagine too much, my love." He gently lowered her fists. "I hear you have extra chores. Want to help me with the rest of my rounds?"

Viviani's eyes flashed from terror to excitement. "Do I!"

Papa grinned. "Let's go, then." He gathered up his toolbox and jerked his head down the hall. "This old girl is counting on us." He patted the cool marble library wall.

They started with his regular chores: winding the clocks, which Papa let Viviani do by herself. It was a single crank that somehow—Viviani thought magic was likely involved—wound every clock in the library at once. It took all her muscle to turn the crank, and her arms burned with the strain. But she felt as if she had incredible powers, being able to control time like that, like in the stories of H. G. Wells about incredible time-traveling machines.

Then they moved to cleaning the pneumatic tubes, a series of clear vacuum tubes that delivered the book requests from the many library desks down into the stacks. A piece of paper *should* whoosh like lightning through the tubes to the massive stacks below the library, but instead, today, the paper inside would float and flutter on a light wind, like a butterfly.

"A clog," Papa declared, and he snaked a long, flexible tube inside until he found the blockage. When they removed it, they saw that an old bird's nest had been lodged inside. "This looks like the work of John Junior and Carroll," Papa said, shaking his head but grinning. "That kid's shenanigans are going to land him either at Harvard or in the pokey."

"My money's on the pokey," Viviani said.

Papa winked. "Don't let your mother hear you placing bets." He checked his list of things to fix. "Monthly elevator maintenance."

Papa pried open the doors on the third-floor elevator, and the empty elevator shaft looked like a subway tunnel direct to the underworld. A waft of old, damp air whooshed out.

Viviani shivered, covered in gooseflesh. The shaft was deep and dark and full of spiderwebs, and the steel cables supporting the cars looked awfully thin when one considered they lifted and lowered thousands of people each day.

Papa swung around the doorframe into the open shaft, clinging to a ladder embedded in the wall. Viviani couldn't help herself; she gasped, seeing her father with nothing but half-inch iron rods sticking out from concrete to support him.

"Hand me that oilcan, Red." Papa's voice boomed out of the elevator shaft, making him sound hollow and ghostly. Viviani gulped. She didn't want to. She really, really didn't want to.

But here's the important part: despite her heart

pounding so loudly that folks on Fifth Avenue could likely hear it, despite feeling positively dizzy when looking down into that gaping, wide hole, she did it.

Viviani Joffre Fedeler knew that courage is simply fear stuffed with hope.

"Next on the list." Papa climbed out of the elevator shaft and tapped his pencil tip against the notepad: "Prep the Stuart Room for the new exhibit. . . ."

"New exhibit?" Viv's eyes lit up. New exhibits meant fancy people in shiny clothes and hats and live music and food and lots of newspaper reporters with popping, smoking flashes. New exhibits were like Hollywood and jazz and flappers swinging their limbs about all in one.

Mama was already inside the Stuart Room, and she gave Viviani a sideways hug. A gaggle of librarians raised quite a fuss in the wide display area in the rear of the room:

"Move the table over there, John. No—yes. There. Now roll in that display case, Alice."

"Oh, my! This area sure is dusty. Are we certain that cleaning crew ever comes in here? What horrible air quality!"

"The air quality is fine," Papa said, shoving a table to make room.

"The dust won't be a problem," said one librarian,

nodding. "But you know what will be? The sunlight. Don't you think it's too much? The skylights are much too bright."

"The skylights are fine," Papa said, hoisting a chair.

"I'm more worried about the moisture in the air. Does it feel humid in here to you? I think it's humid. Have we checked the plumbing nearby?"

"The plumbing is fine." Papa chuckled, unlocking a side closet.

He disappeared in a flurry of table moving and lamplight adjusting. Viviani stood on tiptoe and leaned into the librarians' conversation. Why all the hubbub about the room? "What's coming? Is it alive?"

The group of librarians turned as one toward Viviani. "Alive?" Miss O'Conner asked with a grin. She shoved her glasses up the bridge of her nose.

Viviani shrugged. "Dust. Sunlight. Water. Sounds alive."

"Not alive, but certainly *lively*," came a voice from behind the group. The librarians all tittered and giggled.

Viviani spun. The voice came from Dr. Edwin Hatfield Anderson, the library director. Wowza! Dr. Anderson escorted in only the really important folks. Beside him stood a man whose eyes were masked by tiny, glinting spectacles. When the gentlemen entered, they removed their hats. This was a rule that dated all the way back to Dr. John Shaw Billings, the designer of the library and its original director. This area of the library housed one of the famous Gutenberg Bibles, and Dr. Billings and the other library directors since believed it deserved such respect.

The man beside Dr. Anderson was tall and thin and sharp and pinched. He reminded Viviani of a paper airplane. He carried a large brown briefcase, locked tight.

Locked-tight briefcase *and* Dr. Anderson? This chore was turning less chore-like quickly!

The gentleman, whom Dr. Anderson introduced as Mr. Smyth, snuffled and twitched his nose about, as if tasting the air through his nostrils. He popped his finger in his mouth, then out again, holding his wet pointer finger aloft. His forehead crumpled.

"It's the humidity," one of the librarians whispered, before being elbowed into silence.

Mr. Smyth crouched then, circling the display case. He knocked on the glass. He rattled the case. He bent in half, jerking his head between the case and the skylights, examining the angle of the sun. He snuffled some more.

"What's going on?" Edouard's whisper in Viviani's ear made her yelp. All librarian eyes shot their way, and the group issued a collective *shhhhhhh!* Mama hid a smile behind her hand.

"New display," Viviani whispered back.

"What is it?"

"Dunno. Dr. Anderson says it's 'lively,' though."

Mr. Smyth then bent toward his briefcase and clicked open the shiny brass lock. Viviani noticed how his hands shook diving into the deep case but were steady as stone lions as they lifted out a black velvet-lined tray.

He placed the tray into the glass case. Viviani and Edouard dove forward.

"Stamps?" Viviani said. "That's it? That's lively?"

"Ah, dear girl," said Mr. Smyth as he put another tray in the case. "Not just any stamps. *Rare* stamps."

"There are rare stamps?" Viviani asked. The glare she received in response told her yes, yes, there were.

"Fact," Edouard said. "The world's first postage stamp was known as the Penny Black and came into service on May 6, 1840. Do you have one of those?"

The gentleman unloaded two more trays. "A Penny Black? I wish I did. And, yes, stamps can be rare indeed. This one, for instance," he said, pointing at a stamp featuring a Ferris wheel. "This was to commemorate a World's Fair. Only two hundred ever printed. This is the only one I've ever seen."

"Wow," Edouard said, watching the tray slide into the glass case. Miss O'Conner beamed at him. Viviani thought the librarians would make Edouard their mascot if it were up to them.

Another tray slid into the case. Viviani hung on the glass by her fingertips, trying to get as close as possible to the stamps.

"Don't smudge that case, Viviani," Miss O'Conner warned her. Viv was the opposite of a mascot to the librarians. Viviani thought they saw her more like a lit match, running around the library, all fiery around valuable pieces of paper.

"And this stamp," Mr. Smyth said, cradling a tray like a baby. He pointed his pinkie at a fancy bearded fellow. "This was the last stamp ever printed in the country of Montenegro. After the Great War, that country doesn't even exist anymore."

"Wow," Viviani said. "Do all these belong to you?"

Mr. Smyth smiled. It was a gentle smile, like the soft glow of a candle. "They do. I'm one lucky fellow."

"And we're one lucky library, for you to share your collection with us." Dr. Anderson clamped his hand on Mr. Smyth's shoulder. "That's a ten-thousand-dollar stamp collection right there, kids."

Mr. Smyth flushed red. He obviously didn't think of his collection in terms of dollars, but in a different way entirely: he collected the stories behind the stamps. In a way, he too was a story collector! Viviani knew one when she spotted one.

There were stamps of fancy ladies wearing high, itchy-looking collars. A stamp with the Liberty Bell. Stamps featuring colorful blooming flowers—those were Mama's favorites. A stamp of a hand gripping a sword—that one was Edouard's preference. Viviani considered the fact that this tiny slip of paper, licked and slapped on an envelope, could carry important words and messages and stories to the other side of the world. It seemed so far-fetched when you thought about it—spit on your thoughts, and someone would deliver them worldwide. Magic!

Viviani could see why Mr. Smyth loved his stamps so much. When he handled them, he handled them boldly but gently, with great care. When he spoke of them, his sharpness softened. His paper-airplane edges unfolded and relaxed, like a single smooth page.

"And *this* one," Mr. Smyth said, showing his last tray of stamps to Edouard and Viviani. He pointed at the one in the very center, of a blue airplane. "This one's my prize stamp."

"The airplane is upside down!" Viviani exclaimed.

Mr. Smyth beamed. "Exactly. It's called an Inverted Jenny. In the first batch of stamps, they accidently printed the airplane upside down. But the red frame"—he swept his pinkie fingernail around the edge of the stamp— "was printed right side up. It's a mistake. And after they fixed it, the wrong ones became very valuable."

As Mr. Smyth slid the last tray into the case and Dr. Anderson locked it shut, Viviani's heart swelled. "Oh, wait'll Eva sees this! She'll love it!"

Viviani rushed through the rest of the chores so she could come back to the Stuart Room. She hung on the case, fingerprints smudging the glass, breath fogging the display, and she didn't care because after everyone else left the library for the day, it was just her and these magical slips of paper that deliver words to the world.

The Inverted Jenny was her favorite because it was a mistake. A cherished mistake. If Viviani's many mistakes could be cherished—playing in the workshop, her envious thoughts toward Merit, her note about Mr. Green—why, imagine how appreciated and admired *she'd* be!

CHAPTER NINE

Rites and Ceremonies,

Dewey Decimal 394.21

SEE ALSO: *manners and customs, exhibitions*

The stamp exhibit opened to the public two days later. On the front steps of the library, four postmen in uniform sang barbershop quartet ditties into a large, square metal microphone with the call letters WJZ emblazoned on it, the official library radio station. Cigarette ladies strolled through the crowd, hawking candy and mints. John Jr. followed their lead and tried to sell sticky cups of lemonade to the waiting crowd, but it being a cold November day, he had little success. The men wore fine, gentlemanly hats, and the women wore leather gloves and sharp coats over smart, fringy dresses. Mama made Viviani and the boys dress up for the occasion, too. Viviani was so uncomfortable she thought her dress might very well be made of sandpaper and sawdust, and her shoes fashioned from vise grips from Papa's workshop. She tugged at her starched dress collar and grumbled at her saggy stockings.

The Doughnut Sisters were back, too. Gladys and Irene McIntyre were out on the steps ringing their tiny bells, peddling doughnuts to the crowds.

"You! There! The one about to buy the—"

"—candy! Buy doughnuts instead! Help a cause instead of just—"

"—gaining weight for naught!"

Dr. Anderson welcomed the postmaster of New York City, John J. Kiely, at the top of the wide library steps, between the two center pillars.

"And these stamps are stunning, folks," Dr. Anderson was saying into the WJZ microphone. Viviani could picture listeners as far away as Jersey City tuning in to the station on their boxy home radios. "Stunning. And so rare, the collection is estimated to be worth over ten thousand dollars! Can you imagine?"

The crowd *oohed* and *aahed* for a moment as Dr. Anderson and Postmaster Kiely cut a big red ribbon with a fake pair of oversized scissors. (That was one of the first major disappointments in Viviani's life, finding out that those big scissors were fake and that the ribbon was held together with a dab of glue. Oh, imagine what fun she could have with giant scissors!)

The singing postmen burst into song, and a crowd of several hundred patrons flooded into the building. All these people entering the library, entering Viviani's home. Her chest swelled with pride.

Newspaper flashes popped and smoked, and a reporter approached Viviani. He wore a terrible coat, the color of split pea soup. Split pea soup tasted like mowed grass to Viviani, so she immediately found this fellow distasteful, too.

"Excuse me, miss," he said. "I'd like to hear more about why you're here today."

"I'm here every day."

The reporter looked confused but chuckled. "I mean, I'd like to interview you about this exhibit. What interests you about stamps? I want to hear your story."

Friend, here's where Viviani Fedeler simply froze. Eva had an interesting story to share about her parents escaping Armenia. And Merit could talk about Giza and climbing the pyramids. But Viviani's story?

If this reporter had asked for a story about stamps or had requested facts about the stamps themselves, why, there wouldn't have been enough newsprint in all of

73

New York to publish Viviani's thoughts. But instead, he wanted to know about *her*, and her story. For a split second, Viviani wondered, amid all this glamour and glitz and showmanship, if her part of the story was even worth sharing.

CHAPTER TEN

Errors,

Dewey Decimal 153.4

SEE ALSO: *common fallacies, fallibility, conspiracy theories*

That night, Viviani couldn't sleep. After flopping and flipping and further embellishing her wallpaper, she decided to tiptoe from the apartment and enter the Board of Trustees room directly across the wide hall on the second floor, next door to the administrative offices. It was a quiet room, close enough to the apartment to not truly be considered "wandering," but different enough to distract her buzzy brain. She turned the ornate brass doorknob and slipped inside.

The Board of Trustees room was small by this library's standards, with a low, elaborate ceiling and a carved marble fireplace. Dotting the room were marble busts of people Viviani had to assume were famous.

CRASH!

A clatter from somewhere in the library made Viviani practically leap out of her skin. It sounded like shattering glass.

She snuck back across the hall into the apartment and peeked into John Jr. and Edouard's room; most crashes and clatters seemed to begin with those two. But, no: stinky and dark. She tiptoed to the end of the hallway—her parents both lightly snored in harmony. How was no one else awakened by that noise?

She thought of waking up Papa but could hear his teasing now: "'Twas your imagination—only this and nothing more," he'd say, putting his spin on Poe's famous poem "The Raven."

Viviani creaked open the door of the apartment again—*eeeeEEEEeeee*—and cocked her ear into the silent tomb of a library.

Her heart raced. But no other sound filled the cold, dark building.

Viviani thought of her new commitment to exploration and adventure, then thought of a favorite literary hero, Robert from *Five Children and It*. He and his siblings found a Psammead, and the Sand-fairy granted them all sorts of wonky wishes. Would Robert go back to bed? Or would he explore?

He would most certainly explore.

Viviani placed one slippered foot in front of another, sliding down the hallway without a sound.

The library was silent. Not even Mr. Eames or his jangling keys. If he'd heard something, there would be a huge commotion, right?

Swoosh. Swoosh. Swoosh. She was as quiet as a—

A ghost! Viviani clapped her hand to her mouth.

What if that noise had been Big Red? Papa had said he made up the story, but John Jr. said it was real. Viviani was torn.

Just as the thought of Big Red entered her mind, she heard the tiniest sound: *Tap. Tap. Tap.*

Big Red's hammer!

She peered slowly, cautiously, over the second-story balcony into the massive lobby below. Her heart pounded; her throat was dry. Her eyes adjusted to the dim evening light.

Tap. Tap. Tap.

A long, stretching shadow floated across the floor.

Viviani squeaked, holding in a scream, and skidded and slid all the way back into her apartment—*eeeeEEEEeeee*, went the door—and she ran down the hall and into her room and leapt under her covers, until her heart caught up with her at last and landed back inside her heaving chest.

The next morning before school, Viviani went back and forth, trying to decide if she should tell Papa and the others what she'd heard, what she'd seen. Was it worth the teasing she'd have to endure from John Jr. and Edouard? Finally, she decided it was.

She scurried all over the library, poking her head around corners and bookstacks. "Papa? Papa?" Her voice echoed in many of the rooms, hollow.

Viviani had checked both the third and second floors. As she hopped down the stairs to the first floor, a chill raced over her skin. She got gooseflesh and shivered.

This wasn't uncommon, these unexplained cold spots in the library. They happened all the time, and the administrative staff swore they'd all catch their death because of them. But this sensation, which made her blood run positively cold, was particularly chilling after last night's adventure.

"Papa!" Viviani yelled.

Two librarians passing by below shushed her, out of habit mostly, because the library wasn't even open yet.

Papa must've heard her, though, because he whistled the two-note whistle he had made up for just these moments, when the family needed to find him in this cavernous building: *Twee-TWEE! Twee-TWEE!*

She followed the whistle until she found him near the main entrance. Papa and Mr. Green were bent over the large brass book return where patrons could drop off their books while the library was closed. When Papa straightened, he held a shard of glass, which he placed in a bucket with others. Mr. Green poked open the tiny brass door of the book return to peer outside, and a bright white shaft of sunlight slid in. He dropped the door and turned, scowling when he spotted Viviani. Viviani's stomach flopped. She scowled back. He was the reason she was loaded down with chores lately.

A burning smell stung Viviani's nose, her eyes. The book return stank like kerosene. "What happened?"

Papa shook his head. "Some ne'er-do-well dropped a bottle of moonshine in the book return last night. Ruined thirteen books! I've not seen the librarians this angry in quite some time. Come not between the dragon and her books!"

That had to have been the clatter she heard last night—a glass bottle smashing against the metal of the book return. Viviani exhaled for the first time all morning.

Thank heavens! She smiled and headed back upstairs to ready herself for school. But as she padded up the wide staircase, a troubling thought occurred to her: the crash was now explained away.

But the shadow on the floor and that tapping noise were not.

CHAPTER ELEVEN

Truthfulness & Falsehood,

Dewey Decimal 177.3

SEE ALSO: *deception, honesty*

On their morning walk to school, Eva said, "I'm ready for your punishment to be over. I'm so bored after school! I told you we shouldn't play in your dad's workshop. And we never even got in touch with Martians."

"Oh, sure we did," Viviani said, her words disappearing like ghosts into the gray December sky. She grasped Eva's mittened hand with her own. "I talked to them later. They'll be here in January. They've hitched their horses to their spaceships and are headed this way. They'll be trotting past the moon next week."

Eva laughed.

Viviani winked. "And oh! Just you wait until recess.

I've got a spine chiller of a story to tell today! You'll be terrified!"

"I don't want to hear it."

"Sure you do," Viviani said as she took Eva's hand. She firmly believed that fears were best fought head-on. Courage being fear stuffed with hope and whatnot.

Viviani was convinced that the clocks in her school ran slower than the clocks anywhere else on earth. Geography dragged into spelling dragged into handwriting practice: *AAAAAaaaaa. BBBBBbbbbb. CCCCCccccc.* But at last, *at last*, Miss Hutch said, "Outside, pupils! March, march, march!" Miss Hutch ran her classroom with military precision.

There was a small, dusty yard behind Public School 27, bordering Forty-First Street. The schoolyard was sandwiched between two elevated train stations and was a block and a half from the Edison power houses lining the East River. So it was a noisy yard, full of echoing rumbles and electrical hums and odd, angled shadows. In Viviani's mind, it was the perfect backdrop for her stories.

Viviani had fully intended on sharing her late-night library adventure, the story of the clattering, clanging noise that had woken her up and sent her patrolling the nighttime halls. But throughout the day, the more she thought of that shadow, that tapping sound, and that red-whiskered ghost wandering the halls with his hammer, seeking out mischief and things to smash, the more scared she became. Just the thought of Big Red sent shivers down her spine. And so, peering at the faces gathered before her, awaiting today's tale, she wrung her mittened hands and decided to spin a different yarn.

"Today, friends," she shouted over the sound of a nearby train to the twelve or so kids crowded around, "I want to tell you about the underground river that snakes eerily through the basement of the library, deep below the stacks. If you listen closely when you're in the children's room, you can hear water winding its way to it: *Drip. Drip. Drip.*"

The kids huddled in their overcoats, huffed on their cold hands, and smiled in anticipation. Nobody told a story like Viviani Joffre Fedeler.

"It is a long, slimy river, and some say that a massive, snarling sea monster dwells in its murky depths. And this river—it's *growing*. It gets higher and higher and higher, thanks to a special water source available only to the library: *Drip. Drip. Drip.*"

"How would you know?" came a British-chiseled voice at the edge of the crowd.

The group of kids turned and parted so that Viviani

could see who had asked the question: Merit Mubarak. Merit's golden earrings peeked out from under her knitted cap, and Viviani still thought her pierced ears were maybe the most sophisticated thing this side of the Met.

"I know everything about the library!" Viviani beamed. She hadn't yet had the chance to talk to Merit about being the third musketeer; now was her chance to show her what great friends they'd be.

"But how?" Merit asked again, not quite rudely but with plenty of *oomph*.

"Viviani lives in the library," Eva said.

Merit's forehead wrinkled in disbelief. "What? No one lives in a library."

"I do too live in the library!"

Viv's other classmates nodded as well.

"She does," Laurel Rudolph chimed in.

"Second floor."

"Eight whole rooms—I've seen them! Her and her family."

Merit eyed Viviani, and Viviani felt like one of those bugs pinned to a piece of paper in the library's insect collection. Viviani expected Merit's face to flash a hint of something that said *I'm impressed* or *The library—wow!* but instead, it stayed locked on to *No way*.

"Still," Merit said. "There is no river in the basement."

"There is!" Viviani declared, because there *could* be.

Viviani was getting flustered because Merit obviously didn't understand how stories *work*. Their truth was in their fun, not in their facts. Viviani watched as the other kids began to mutter to each other. Some of them shifted as if ready to walk away.

Viviani thought quickly. That constant dripping sound had to lead to something, didn't it? It had even been a reservoir once. Water once filled up her papa's workshop.

Her papa's workshop! That *must* go in the story.

"Next to the river," Viviani continued, "are the *dungeons*."

"Dungeons?" a kid asked.

Eva hid her grin behind her mitten. She was picturing the workshop, too. Viviani was sure of it.

"Yes, the dungeons. They're used by those spiteful librarians and filled with, with—tools!"

"Tools?" Merit arched an eyebrow.

"Tools!" Viviani declared, finger aloft. She was really spinning a good yarn now. "Saws and drills and clamps! The librarians save them for the cheats who don't return their library books on time, or for those scoundrels who dog-ear the pages, or for the toddlers who draw in books! They become prisoners, all of them!"

Viviani almost cracked herself up. Babies were

85

cuddled like cherubs by every librarian in the building during story time, and the collected late fees paid for some nice things for the library. But those wouldn't make for a very fun story. Viviani could see that she had won the crowd again.

"So if you have body parts that can be sawed or drilled or clamped"—she pointed to her audience, some of whom giggled, some of whom shivered—"you'd best return your books on time. Because you know why there's a slimy, long underground river?"

She paused, for pausing is a great tool of storytellers.

Finally Eva, ever her trusted partner, said, "Why?"

"It's the tears of the prisoners!" Here, she pretended to sob, muttering, "*Drip. Drip. Drip.*"

Viviani's schoolyard audience clapped. All but one.

"Rubbish," Merit said.

"Is not!" Viviani yelled.

"Then show me," Merit said. "Show me the river. I want to see those dungeons."

The crowd gasped. Viviani fumbled. "You can't go down there," she said to the ground.

"And why not?" Merit demanded.

"You just can't." Viviani didn't want to admit that she'd just been scolded for going into the basement. She also didn't want to admit that after hearing her papa's story, she didn't *care* to go into the basement. Just the thought of Big Red made her hair stand on end. Viviani felt downright comfortable sharing a story she knew to be creepy but false. Sharing a story she considered creepy but *true* felt terrifying.

"Why?"

Viviani's voice shook in a way that made her angry at herself. "There's a ghost down there. A red-whiskered ghost. With a hammer."

Eva's eyes widened. "A what? You never told me about a ghost, Viv." Her fingers knotted. Viviani knew she was thinking of the shadow they'd seen in the hallway when they were being inventors.

Merit's eyes narrowed. "Of course she didn't, Eva. Because it isn't true. The ghost, the river, the dungeons— none of it is true."

"It is true! The librarians, the staff—everybody! They all know about him. They call him Big Red."

"Red?" Jake Joseph smirked. "Isn't that what your family calls you? Red?" The rest of the crowd shuffled and mumbled.

"Yeah, that's *your* nickname."

"I've heard them say it."

"Can't you see?" Merit said. "She's lying." She huffed and crossed her arms. "Viviani Joffre Fedeler is a liar."

CHAPTER TWELVE

Collectors & Collecting,

Dewey Decimal 790.1

SEE ALSO: *collectibles, hobbies*

Being labeled a liar is a little like being labeled a person who has infectious cooties. At the word *liar*, Viviani's classmates scattered as if they were avoiding lice. Viviani slunk to a bench, Eva by her side. But Viv saw Eva's fingers twitch as some kids scratched a marble arena into the dirt with a stick across the way. Eva was a deadeye at marbles; no one could beat her, and she had won all the best ones.

"Go on," Viviani said, lifting her chin at the game.

"You sure?"

"I'm sure," Viviani said.

Eva stood, dug a stick of Juicy Fruit gum from her pocket, and tore it in half. She gave half to Viv, then bolted, the marbles in her pockets clacking. "Wait for me!"

Viviani popped the gum in her mouth. It was stale.

Can a person feel like chewed, flavorless gum?

Because Viviani felt like chewed, flavorless gum.

After school that day, and after chores after that, Viviani went to the map room to cheer herself up. But all the krakens and all the sea dragons and all the giant squid in the world couldn't wash away her bad mood. So she marched up two flights of stairs to see the Inverted Jenny.

What it must be like to fly! Far above the rooftops, far into the clouds, far away from words like *liar* and the giggles of the others when Merit called her that. The very idea of it made her breathless.

Through the fingerprint-smudged, fogged-up glass of the display case, Viviani spotted a familiar face. Rather, a familiar coat. A horrid pea-soup coat. "Hey, you're that reporter!"

As it was almost closing time for the library, the gentleman in the terrible coat was the only other patron in the room looking at the stamps. His head shot up, but his eyebrows shot down. "Excuse me?"

"The day this exhibit opened. You asked me some

questions. But I—" Viviani didn't want to admit she had been at a loss for words when he'd asked about her. "Hey! What's it like to be a reporter? Have you met any celebrities? I bet you have! Oh! You've met Buster Keaton, haven't you? Did Buster tell you all about his gags and stunts and pratfalls?"

The man in the pea-soup coat shook his head. "I—"

"Or are you a restaurant critic? Those fellas have the best job. What's your favorite restaurant in the city? My brother's friend Carroll? His dad is the chef at the Algonquin Hotel. Have you eaten there? It's fancy."

The man's face lifted slightly into a grin. "Well, I—"

"Or do you report on bad guys? Gangsters and bootleggers and whatnot? Do you know Al Capone's secret handshake? Can you teach it to me?"

The man circled the glass case with all the rare, valuable stamps inside. "Has anyone ever told you you're like a real-life Anne of Green Gables?"

Viviani's shoulders slumped. "Yes. All the time. She asks too many questions."

"What? No. She's the bee's knees!" the man in the pea-soup coat said. He had a slanted grin. "She has quite the imagination, and she'll believe just about anything!"

"Sounds pretty gullible to me."

The man laughed. "Do you make up stories for everyone you meet?"

Viviani shrugged. "I guess so. I just have so many questions about everyone, and Mama says it's rude to ask someone thirty questions when you first meet them. Go figure."

"Go figure."

Viviani smiled. "Everyone else's stories all seem so . . . *interesting*, that's all. I just want to fill in the blanks."

"Noble work, that." The man in the pea-soup coat nodded and narrowed his eyes at Viviani. And so Viviani narrowed her eyes back.

"You're here a lot?" he asked. "At the library, I mean."

"I live here."

The man's face lit up. "No!"

His no made Viviani smile despite herself. For his wasn't an *I don't believe you* no. A no like that sounds sharp and quick, like a scissor slice. Rather, this was an incredulous no, a *WOW, really?* breathless kind of no. This gentleman's no was filled with awe. Funny how two small letters can communicate so many different meanings, no?

"I do! My papa's the superintendent."

"You don't say."

Viviani folded her arms across her chest and thrust her chin skyward. "I do so say." The man's laugh echoed about the cavernous, quiet space. Viviani decided she could forgive him his terrible taste in coats.

A librarian poked her head in the Stuart Room. "Five minutes, folks. The library closes in five minutes."

The fellow extended his hand for a handshake. "What's your real name, Anne Shirley?"

Viviani gripped the gentleman's hand. "Viviani Joffre Fedeler. At your service, and always at the ready with a good yarn."

"I don't doubt it. I'm Mr. Uh . . . Hill," he said, touching the brim of his hat.

"Quite a first name you got there, Uh!" Viviani laughed. The fellow did as well.

Mr. Hill jerked his head at the collection. "Are you a stamp collector?"

Viviani shook her head. "No. I just like the stories behind them. I'm a . . . a story collector."

The man smiled ear to ear. "A story collector. I like that." They stood in silence for a moment more, admiring the tiny, colorful stamps.

"What do you collect?" Viviani asked the fellow. "Oh! Lemme guess. Arrowheads! No. Baseball cards! No. Coins!"

The man didn't look up from the glass display case. He sighed deeply. "Me? I collect bad luck."

CHAPTER THIRTEEN

Lying,

Dewey Decimal 363.25

SEE ALSO: *falsehoods, tall tales*

After her encounter with Mr. Uh Hill, who seemed charmed by the fact that she loved stories, Viviani asked herself: Is there a difference between a liar and a storyteller?

That's one of those tricky questions one must answer for oneself. It depends, doesn't it, on the situation, on the story, on the intent, on the person? Viviani knew her intentions were good—why couldn't Merit see that? Unlike books, people cannot be neatly assigned a Dewey decimal number and lined up on a shelf in an orderly manner.

The more Big Red slunk through Little Red's mind, hammer in fist, the more Viviani completely, totally, and thoroughly believed in him. And when she had tried to talk to Eva about it, the one person who had *seen* Big Red with her, Eva just shook her head furiously. "I don't wanna talk about that, Viv. It's too scary."

Eva was not turning this *could* into *impossible*, as Viviani had hoped she would.

Viviani thought ghosts were not only possible but probable, so why not *here*, in the library? The more she thought about it, she'd even *seen* it. Sort of. It *could* be true.

Perhaps Viviani was so fond of *could*s because Papa was an inventor, and inventors by their very nature see the world as it *could* be. Inventors are fond of saying things such as, "Whether you think you can or think you can't, you're right." Henry Ford, the American automobile manufacturer, said that. Or: "I have not failed. I've just found ten thousand ways that won't work." That one was from Papa's friend Thomas Edison.

Between her father's inventor idealism and her natural proclivity for stories, Viviani Joffre Fedeler was able to see fiction in a slightly more true light than most. Merit's doubts and finger-pointing earlier felt a little bit like a hammer, chipping away at Viviani's sincerity.

In class the following day, Laurel Rudolph leaned way over in her desk and poked Viviani in the arm with her pen nib. "What are some of the weird things that library ghost does?" she whispered.

"Well, sometimes piles of books will mysteriously appear on the floor where someone had walked just five minutes before," Viviani whispered back, and the two kids seated next to Laurel shuddered. "There won't be a crash, no loud noise, just a stack of books where there wasn't one a moment ago."

Laurel gasped and was quickly shushed by Miss Hutch.

On the way to the restroom that morning, Helen Hoogland murmured over her shoulder to Viv, "Say, that ghost—it ever touch anybody?"

Viviani nodded. "Sometimes the librarians say they feel someone—or *something*—stroking their hair. Something very cold. Slimy."

The nearby classmates in the line for the restroom shuddered and whispered in delight.

Miss Hutch quieted them down.

And out in the schoolyard at recess, James Ziegler asked, "Does the ghost moan? You know, you ever hear anything odd?"

"Besides Big Red's hammer?" Viviani asked, and Jake Goodman smiled and nudged Cory Stout. Was it because he believed her, or was it in jest? "Sure. Creaking doors, and footsteps, and—"

"All of those things can be explained by the fact that you live in a library," Merit interrupted. Her arms crossed her chest; her toe tapped. "People coming and going all the time."

"And *sometimes*, the librarians say, they hear crying," Viviani said loudly.

"Crying?" Eva's fingers knotted.

Viviani swallowed, her throat dry. "Crying. Like a child who lost his mother." Her classmates were wide-eyed and listening. She was winning them back!

"Book carts will roll down the aisle slowly—*v e r y* slowly, mind you—so that you wouldn't even notice them moving, except you're *sure* they aren't where they were fifteen minutes before. Lights flicker all the time, on off, on off. Typewriter keys clacking, but no typewriter is in use. And once"—here Viviani gulped—"a single book flew off a shelf, narrowly missing a patron's head."

All of this was true, mind you, to the degree that all these things had indeed been reported in the library. Viviani had done some digging recently, trying to decide if Big Red was real, and had been told all of the above. But, Edouard had reminded her, just because these things were *reported* doesn't mean they're actually *true*. Sometimes people just want to feel like they're a part of a bigger story.

Viviani's classmates huffed warm, wet clouds onto their cold hands and shivered with the deliciousness of it all. Everyone except Merit. Her huffs looked more like a storybook dragon's.

"Malarkey," said Merit. "All of these things happened to *you*, Viviani?"

"No, but—"

"Who did they happen to?"

"Librarians, like I said. Patrons. Other library workers."

Merit's lips knotted as if they were yanked by a single string to the side of her face. "That's all ghost stories are—someone thinking they saw something or heard something, when it's just their imagination running away with them." Here, she arched an eyebrow at Viviani. "Imaginations can be dangerous."

"Well, yeah! Without imagination, *nothing* is dangerous," Viviani shot back. "Danger is just your brain imagining the worst that could happen and hopping up and down and shouting, *Warning! That could hurt you!*" Now *her* arms were crossed and *her* eyebrows furrowed.

How could two people agree and yet still see things so differently?

It seemed their classmates could feel how strongly the two girls repelled each other, as if they were two like ends of a magnet. And Viviani noticed by the looks on some of their faces that not everyone agreed with her. It was surprising and hurtful.

"What a load of applesauce," Cory muttered as Viviani turned to walk away.

"She's all wet," Jake agreed.

Viviani felt her chin begin to tremble. *Not here*, she told herself. *Do NOT cry here.* She raised her face to the low gray sky.

Snow began to fall in fat, soft flakes, so recess story time quickly became recess snow time, with snowmen and snow angels and catching snowflakes on tongues. Viviani grew numb from the cold as she watched the fun around her.

The rest of the day, Viviani sat at her desk, damp with snow but steaming from the too-hot radiator. It was a woeful combination, coupled with the misery she felt from knowing some of her classmates doubted her. Even Eva's little jokes couldn't cheer her up.

After school, several kids played in Bryant Park, just behind the library, in the deep, wet new-fallen snow. Viviani decided her mood could use the boost that only a good old-fashioned snowball fight could provide. She and Eva quickly joined forces with John Jr. and Carroll behind their snow fort near the courtyard fountain. They packed an arsenal of small, tight snowballs.

Someone on the other team pointed up at a window on the back side of the library: a long, thin window that showcased the seven tiers of heavy iron bookstacks.

"Look!" he shouted. It was Jake Joseph from Viviani's class. "It's Big Red!"

Viviani couldn't help herself: the itch of story, the pull of *could* was simply that strong for her. She stood, turned, and faced the library to get a glimpse of the red-whiskered ghost.

Whack!

A snowball walloped the back of her head, bits of ice dripping and sliding down her neck and into the collar of her dress.

"Ha!" Jake yelled. "Look at that! I lied, too!"

Normally, Viviani would let out a hoot and lob a snowball back, but today, her shoulders sagged. She shook the snow out of her coat and let her snowballs fall to the ground.

"What a sap," John Jr. said. "I'll get him."

Viviani appreciated the promise with a small nod. She looked at Eva, who raised eyebrows as if to ask, *Want me to come, too?* Viviani shook her head. She wanted to be alone.

Without another word, Viviani dragged her feet through the snow in Bryant Park, leaving long, lonely tracks behind her.

CHAPTER FOURTEEN

Data,

Dewey Decimal 005.8

SEE ALSO: *data mining, data collection*

Viviani didn't feel like going back to her room; if she did, she'd just sit there and sulk and wallow, and that sounded like exactly as much fun as guzzling pickle juice. She knew just who she needed to find. But finding him inside the library wasn't always easy. If Viviani saw the library as her playground, Edouard Fedeler saw the library as his cathedral, and he was usually as silent as a church mouse (which made him the frequent monthly winner at Master Thief, naturally).

Inside the apartment, Viv grabbed a Charleston Chew and found her mother humming along to Duke Ellington and prepping flyers for her League of Women Voters meeting. "Edouard here?"

Her mother shook her head. "Try the auditorium."

Viviani stuffed the sticky candy into her mouth and wound her way down to the first floor. According to the poster outside the door, the lecture was called "Patent Medicine Frauds." Viviani poked her head inside and shout-whispered, "Edouard? Are you here?" The entire audience plus speaker scowled at the interruption, and she backed out of the room, surprised Edouard wasn't there. Patent medicine frauds sounded right up his nonfiction aisle.

She checked the genealogy room. No Edouard. The art and architecture room. No Edouard. The American history room. No Edouard. At last, she found him in the glass WJZ radio booth on the basement floor, arguing about the merits of jazz with Tommy Cowan, the radio announcer.

"But it's a perfect evolution of American music," Edouard was saying.

"Yes, however—" Mr. Cowan began, but suddenly the album that was playing skipped and skipped and skipped again. He held up a *Quiet, please* finger and flipped a switch on his microphone. "Sorry about that, listeners," he said in a buttery tone. "Sometimes this music simply gets ahead of itself! Please enjoy this selection of chamber music from the Lenox String Quartet." He deftly replaced the scratched record with a new one, and the music rolled out over the airwaves again. He flipped the microphone off.

"I agree about the importance of the jazz movement," Mr. Cowan continued, his voice far more nasal when he wasn't crooning into a microphone. "But if I get caught playing something like Willie Smith? That'd be my head, ya know?" He ran his finger across his throat.

"Chicken."

The announcer nodded. "Absolutely. I absolutely am too chicken to try that."

"Ed, Mama needs you," Viviani interrupted.

Edouard stood and followed Viviani into the hallway. "What does Mama need?"

"What? Oh, nothing. I just had a question. Can I ask you something, Ed?"

"You just did." Edouard sighed. "But you can ask me something else. If you don't call me Ed."

Viviani looked over both shoulders to see who might be nearby. Only a couple of patrons deep in their browsing. "Do you . . . believe in ghosts?"

Edouard stopped walking. Scratched his chin. "I haven't decided. There's plenty of empirical evidence to suggest they exist."

Viviani shivered. Was that another cold spot? Edouard was the one person she was counting on to tell her ghosts were nothing but pure bunk! Not that she wanted Merit to be right about the unlikelihood of ghosts, of course, but the alternative meant there could be an actual *ghost* in her *house*. "What do you mean?"

He tapped his fingertips together, a sign that he was in deep thought. "Well, logically, I'd dismiss the idea outright. I mean, spirits wandering the earth after death? Certainly our spirits have better things to do!" He chuckled, and Viviani forced a weak smile to keep him talking.

"But if you look at the data: over a fifth of the population claims to have seen a ghost. That seems high, doesn't it? Surely not all those people are unreasonable."

Viviani's ears began to ring. What was Edouard saying?

"And that's nothing compared to the percentage of people who say they *believe* in ghosts. Almost half. I can't imagine that much of the population believes in something that doesn't exist."

Viviani gulped. "So," she whispered, "you *do* believe?"

Edouard shrugged. "I usually trust data."

That did it. If Edouard—facts-are-everything, prove-it-to-me Edouard—thought ghosts might exist, then they absolutely, most certainly, positively did. This *could* was a *definitely*.

CHAPTER FIFTEEN

Public Libraries—United States,
Dewey Decimal 027.4

SEE ALSO: *libraries & society; libraries & community; library users*

Viviani marched through the next few days, feeling the glares of her classmates boring through her. She heard their whispered giggles as she passed: "She's full of baloney" and "She told me she was even born *in* the building. I bet that's not true." Eva would grab her hand and pull her through and past the whispers. It was just like walking through the unexplainable cold spots in the library, Viv felt.

Merit didn't join in the gossip, Viviani noticed, but she was the reason people were talking about her. And Merit still didn't believe Viv's library adventures, either.

Every day, Viviani dashed home to do her chores, then lingered by the stamps and the Inverted Jenny.

Viv would love to have Eva by her side in the afternoons, too, leading the way toward the warmer spots in the world, but Viv was still working off her workshop punishment, so . . . no Eva. Instead, Viv would look at the botched stamp and dream of flying around the world, upside down or right side up—it didn't matter, as long as she went far and fast. Like Charles Lindbergh. And every day, Mr. Uh Hill in the terrible pea-soup coat was there, too.

Today, he asked, "How's the story collecting going, Anne Shirley?"

Viviani wished her dress had pockets like the ones her brothers had in their breeches; she had nowhere to cram her balled fists. "Maybe story collecting isn't as nifty as I thought it was."

Mr. Hill looked taken aback. "Of course it is! I think it might be the very best type of collecting."

Viviani shrugged. She didn't feel like talking about her schoolyard troubles now. She came to the library to avoid that. "How's the bad-luck collecting?"

"Going quite well, unfortunately." Mr. Hill let out a rueful chuckle.

A passing librarian, Mr. Wilburforce, shushed them.

Viviani sighed. "Free shushing," she shout-whispered to Mr. Hill. "Comes with the house."

Mr. Hill spit out a laugh. He quickly turned it into a

cough when Mr. Wilburforce eyed him again. "That could really get annoying."

"Plenty of places to hide from those librarians, that's for sure."

"Yeah?" The man's eyes sparkled, like he wanted in on the secret. "So where's the best hiding spot in the building?"

Viviani's heart leapt, for there was nothing she adored more than talking about the library. It felt good to be believed. "You wanna see it?"

"You bet."

"Come on!" Viviani took off at a full run, her shoes slapping the marble floors, escorted out the door by Mr. Wilburforce's shushes. Her fellow collector had to hustle to keep up. When they reached the stairs, Viviani slung one leg over the wooden banister and slid down. Such theatrics were sometimes worth the scowls from the librarians.

Mr. Hill jogged down the flight of stairs. "Just how many floors are there?" he asked, his breath coming in quick puffs.

"Four. Three and the basement. But half of the basement is off-limits."

"Off-limits?"

"Yeah, where the furnace and my papa's workshop are. No one's allowed down there. Not even me."

They slid and ran down two more flights, to the "in bounds" part of the basement, as Edouard liked to call it.

"The children's room, the lunchroom, the newspapers, the bindery, the staff lockers, the Printing Office, the big bookstacks, and the library school," Viviani rattled off. "All here in the basement. Come on, I'll show you the best hiding spot."

Mr. Hill followed Viviani into the room where the library school was housed, a large room with desks and shelves and one massive card catalog, at least ten feet tall.

"Okay, watch this," Viviani said. She pulled out several of the long, skinny wooden drawers in a box pattern, as high as she could reach. The drawers were filled with slips of cardstock, each typed with book information, ready for the library students to learn shelving and weeding and the Dewey decimal system.

Viviani gripped one of the extended drawers and pulled herself aloft. She began to climb. As she did, she tucked in each drawer behind her with the toe of her boot, and she pulled out a drawer above her. Open drawer above, climb, close drawer below. Open drawer above, climb, close drawer below. She climbed to the top of that ten-foot chest of drawers like a spider, and because she closed the drawers behind her, no one could tell she'd been there.

When Viviani reached the top of the card catalog, she flipped onto the flat upper surface and lay down. "You can't see me, can you?" she yelled to Mr. Hill.

She heard him chuckle from below. "Not at all! That's amazing, Viviani!"

She peeked her head over the edge. "Getting down's a little trickier." Viviani performed the action in reverse, this time climbing down and pulling open the card catalog drawers using the tiny brass hooks on the front of each—a perfect fit for the toe of her boot.

When she was low enough, she hopped to the ground and dusted off her hands. Mr. Hill whistled, long and low. "Impressive!"

Viviani took a bow. "Want to see more of the library?"

"Sure!"

As the duo circled out of the library school room and down the corridor, they passed a heavy metal door. Mr. Hill pounded on it, and the hallway filled with a hollow, echoing sound, like thunder.

"What's behind here?"

Viviani paused and could almost hear the *drip drip drip* sound on the other side of that door. Papa's workshop was over there. The furnace. The machine room. The custodian closet. Big Red?

"I'm not allowed to go in there," she said, hiding a shiver. Just standing this close to the spot where she'd seen the swishing shadow and felt pins and needles on her skin, made her heart skip to a faster beat. She leaned closer to Mr. Hill and whispered, "It's haunted."

Viviani glanced sidewise at him to gauge his reaction. He didn't twitch. "Well, we shouldn't stay long here, then. I'd prefer not to have a run-in with a ghost today, thank you very much."

Viviani smiled. *This* fellow didn't call her a liar for believing in ghosts.

"Want to see the roof?" Viviani asked.

"Absolutely."

They jogged back upstairs. At the first-floor landing, Viviani said, "First floor! Maps, magazines, and microfilm! And oh! Mr. Eames! I'd almost forgotten!" She quickly flattened herself against the cool marble wall and scooted out of the security guard's view. It was late afternoon, almost dinnertime, so Mr. Eames had just come on duty. One had to be ever mindful of the Master Thief point tally. John Jr. was now in the lead. Mr. Eames jangled and whistled on by, today sporting a bow tie festooned with holly leaves.

Mr. Hill grinned. "Don't those security guards wake you up at night with all their stomping around?"

"Naw. We never hear them. I sometimes wonder if Mr. Eames doesn't have a nap pallet laid out somewhere. We know his routine backward and forward.

First floor, left turn, full circle, repeat. And he never takes the stairs. Always the elevator for that fellow. That over there is my brother Edouard." Viviani pointed at an open book gripped by a set of fingers. "As you can see, he's annoying," Viviani teased.

Edouard slouched inside a wooden telephone booth, his sock feet propped far above his head, like an over-turned turtle.

"Hello, Edouard!" Mr. Hill called.

"*You're* annoying!" Edouard said, not even looking up from his book.

"This is Mr. Hill," Viviani said. "He wants to see the roof."

Edouard slammed his book shut and tossed it on the bench in the telephone booth. "I wanna come."

The trio ran up the second flight of stairs. Here Viviani said, "Floor two! Mostly art here. Also, one of the biggest card catalogs. And, of course, my home. So, the boring stuff."

Mr. Hill chuckled at that. "What time is lights-out?"

"Ten o'clock. Those iron front doors close shut *boom!* And then the building is all ours."

"And then you have the place all to yourself? Lucky you!"

"Yes. Well, except for Mr. Eames, of course. Oh, and old Mr. Green." Viviani shivered. "He's the custodian.

Cleans up after everyone leaves. You don't want to mess with him."

Mr. Hill nodded like he understood folks you don't mess with.

"Fact," Edouard said as they continued climbing. "The word *librarian* comes from the term *custodian of a library*."

After the third flight of stairs, Viviani said, "Back where we started. This floor has the genealogy room and the fancy picture gallery and the American history room. And, of course, the Main Reading Room."

They entered the main reading room through the grand double wooden doors. The gold inscription carved in wood above the doors greeted them: *A good Booke is the precious life-blood of a master spirit, imbalm'd and treasur'd up on purpose to a life beyond life.*

Viviani's eyes gleamed a little brighter whenever she paused to read those words from the poet John Milton. The script was clean but the *S*s looked more like *F*s, which made the message feel ancient, important. Books were the *life-blood of a master spirit*—Viviani felt pretty sure that meant that books feed your soul. And stories gave a *life beyond life*. That was what Viviani loved most about stories—they made things more exciting, more simple, more straightforward than real life. In stories, there was a beginning, a middle, and an end. They happened Once Upon a Time and usually ended Happily Ever After. Stories helped make sense of big feelings and unexplainable things. Story life was so much more appealing than real life, where things were messy and complicated and people called you *liar*.

"I love this room," Mr. Hill said. The trio stood for a moment taking in the glittering globe chandeliers, the deep, chocolate-brown plasterwork, the gold inlay, the soft green lighting. One could practically *feel* the stories changing hearts and opening minds within the walls of the reading room. Empathy in flight. If ever a place held magic, it was this place.

"Come on," Viviani said. "This way to the roof."

After one last flight of stairs, they reached the door to the roof at last. Viviani paused dramatically, then flung open the metal door with a loud "Ta-da!"

A burst of cold stung their eyes and noses. The pigeons flustered up inside their cages, spraying a cloud of feathers and dander.

Edouard scooped a few handfuls of seed from a nearby bucket and tossed it in their cages. Viviani joined him. "My brother John had the idea to trap pigeons so he can sell them. He built these contraptions out of old parts from my papa's workshop. They look awful, but they work! He's captured twelve so far. He says pigeons carried messages in the Great War, so he thinks he can get a pretty penny for them."

"Sell pigeons in New York?" Mr. Hill said with a half smile. "There's not exactly a shortage of them around here."

"That's what I said!" Viviani cried.

"Pigeons have excellent hearing," Edouard said, peering into the birdcages. "They can detect storms and even volcano eruptions miles away."

"Seems you kids have benefited quite well from living in a library."

Viviani stepped to the edge of the building and swept her arm over the view: the green swath of Bryant Park, the red-tile rooftops and steeples hopping and dotting across Fifth to Sixth Avenue, from east to west. She turned to Forty-Second and Fortieth, north to south, all the way down to the gleaming white spire of the towering Woolworth Building in the distance. The sun was setting pink, turning the East River to her left and the Hudson on her right into pathways of sparkling diamonds. Lights and streets glittered like a universe—the whole New York City universe.

"Isn't the view grand?" She turned to Mr. Hill in his terrible pea-soup coat.

He was spinning, taking in the entirety of the roof. "It is, Viviani. It is grand indeed. Thank you for showing me this."

Viviani smiled. Even if her classmates didn't always appreciate her home, some folks sure did.

CHAPTER SIXTEEN

Cameras,

Dewey Decimal 770

SEE ALSO: *photography, photography—technique*

It was show-and-tell day in Viviani's class. Many of her classmates thought they were too old for show-and-tell, but Viviani still loved this day, for it was story-sharing at its core.

"And that's the story of the Inverted Jenny," Viviani said, snapping shut the book she'd borrowed from the library. It had a picture of the stamp inside. Viviani had a library card just like everyone else, but she rarely remembered to use it before borrowing a book, much to Miss O'Conner's dismay.

"Wow," Merit breathed from her desk. "So interesting. It's valuable because it was a mistake."

Viviani beamed and was, admittedly, a tiny bit surprised. "Exactly!"

"Thank you, Miss Fedeler," her teacher said. Her classmates applauded. "Let's see. Miss Mubarak. How about you go next?"

Merit strolled to the front of the class, clutching a small black box. She flipped a silver handle on the front of it, and out popped a lens and a tiny eyepiece.

"This is our camera," Merit said proudly. The class all leaned forward in their seats, causing the desks and chairs to make a collective *screech* across the cold linoleum floor.

"Wow!"

"Wouldja lookit that!"

"Nifty!"

Viviani felt a surge of jealousy; only Merit had thought her stamp was all that nifty.

"My father bought it back in Giza so we could take pictures of my home before we left."

Here, Viviani noticed a small pause in Merit's story, a slight shake in her voice. But Merit swallowed and continued:

"I took pictures of our journey here. The ship, the water. I even have photographs of us at Ellis Island and the Statue of Liberty!"

The classmates *oohed* and *aahed*.

"But I don't take many pictures, of course. It costs a lot of money to buy film and develop the photographs. Ten dollars per roll."

Wow. That was gobs of money.

"How does it work?" Ruth O'Donnell shouted.

Miss Hutch cleared her throat. "Raise your hand if you have a question, please."

Ruth shot her hand in the air and shouted, "How does it work?"

Merit laughed, and Viviani noticed how it changed her: her shoulders relaxed, her face lit up, her stance softened. Much like the stamp collector Mr. Smyth. Merit had found the hobby that made her melty.

"Well, you focus it here," she said, pointing to the small lens. "And then you push this button here." She turned the camera and showed the class the silver button on top. "The film goes in here." She flipped the case and pointed to the back. "I want to be a newspaper photographer someday, like Christina Broom, who took a lot of photos of soldiers in Britain in the war."

Jake Joseph shot his hand in the air, and Merit nodded at him. "Did you borrow that from your brother?"

Merit's forehead crinkled. "No. I don't have a brother."

"But cameras are for boys. My Boy Scout manual has a section all about photography."

Merit folded the accordion-like lens back into the hard-shell box and closed the case with a *click*. "I hardly think this camera knows if it's a boy or a girl pushing the button."

Viviani couldn't help herself: she burst out laughing. Merit toed the floor with her boot and fought back a grin.

Sometimes a glimpse of sunshine makes itself known through the murky leaves and limbs of the dark forest. Sometimes a glimmer of friendship can be found in places where only animosity was seen before.

Miss Hutch cleared her throat. "That's wonderful, Miss Mubarak. Thank you. Time for recess, kids. March, march, march."

Viviani's class stampeded outside. Some took up a ball and bat. Some played jacks or cards. Viviani wandered to the crowd surrounding Merit, where several friends were still asking about her camera. Viviani felt a small flicker inside, like maybe a spark of friendship. Merit understood the importance of the Inverted Jenny, too.

"That camera really is something," Viviani interrupted.

Merit smiled at her through the throng. "Thank you, Viviani. I really love taking pictures."

Viviani nodded. "Because then you have all your adventures and memories saved forever."

Merit blinked and shook her head ever so slightly. "Yes, but that's not why I like it. I like it because photographs capture the truth. You can't lie on film. Not like you can in stories."

Viviani felt heat rise behind her cheeks. Here was Merit, calling her a liar *again*. And after Viviani had been so nice to her. Their classmates apparently caught that, too, because murmurs and giggles rippled through the crowd.

And so once again, Viviani's mouth said words before her brain had finished thinking them. "Why don't you come to the library for a sleepover during winter break? You can bring that camera to capture a picture of Big Red. The library once had a whole exhibit on spirit photography. Maybe you can photograph our ghost."

"Oh," a classmate whispered.

"Impossible," said another.

"That sounds dangerous," Eva chimed in.

Merit smiled. "Excellent idea. If my camera caught a picture of Big Red, then I'd believe you. Photographs never lie."

Viviani's heart sank. The glimmer of friendship she thought she'd seen earlier got snuffed out like a candle, and all that was left was smelly, smoky char. Just when Viviani was starting to like Merit, Merit had to go and make herself unlikable again.

"Good, I'll see you there." Viviani walked off with her head held high, but her stomach knotted with worry. Winter break was only two days away. The very idea of trying to capture a photo of Big Red made her insides feel all twisty. Sure, Viviani had seen shifting shadows, felt cold shivers, and heard strange drips and thumps and bumps that could be a hammer, but a photograph couldn't capture that. Could a ghost like Big Red even be photographed?

Viviani knew if a ghost *didn't* appear, she'd be branded a liar for sure. No one would ever listen to her stories again.

At the sound of the school bell, Viviani cracked her knuckles and muttered to herself, "Well, I guess I'm going to have to give her something to photograph, then."

Eva, ever close, overheard Viviani's mutterings. "That *definitely* sounds dangerous."

CHAPTER SEVENTEEN

Journal Keeping,
Dewey Decimal 808.02

SEE ALSO: *diary authorship*

Viviani tapped her forehead. She had a big puzzle to solve, maybe the biggest she'd ever had to figure out. *How does one summon a ghost?*

Viviani did all the things that usually got her brain ticking. She paced the long aisles between stacks of musty-smelling books, running her fingers over their dusty leather spines. She zipped her fingernails over the cards in the card catalog, skipped rope in the map room, and tipped upside down into a handstand against the circulation desk, leaving footprints on the carved wooden wall. She conversed with the dozens of oil portraits hanging in the galleries: "Emma Dorothy Eliza

Nevitte Southworth, you made up lots of stories. What do you think I should do?" "Ben, did you ever get yourself into such a pickle?" "George—I can call you that, right, General Washington? George, I could use some of that wisdom of yours right now."

But nothing clicked into place. She decided to visit the Inverted Jenny for inspiration, but when she got there, she wasn't alone.

"Viviani! How's the story collecting going?" Mr. Hill smiled.

Viviani scowled. "I'm quitting that."

Mr. Hill blinked. "I'm not so sure it's a choice."

It was Viviani's turn to blink. "What do you mean?"

"You could argue the objects choose the collector, as much as the collector chooses the objects. Just like I can't help but collect bad luck!"

Viviani's scowl deepened further still. One might even call it a pucker. "Maybe your bad luck has rubbed off on me. Lately my stories have gotten me nowhere good. I've decided I'm quitting stories."

"I'm sorry to hear that." Mr. Hill shook his head. Then he brightened. "But I have just the thing!" He reached into the pocket of his terrible green coat and pulled out a book.

"Another story? That's not exactly what a story quitter needs, Mr. Hill."

Mr. Hill flipped open the book and held it out to Viviani. "Not a book. A *blank* book. This one's for *your* story, Viviani."

Viviani eyed the blank pages and felt her stomach tighten. Would she even have a story worth telling? One that wouldn't land her in a heap of trouble?

Mr. Hill seemed to understand her hesitation. "Think of it like a diary."

"Me? Keep a diary? Not this girl."

"I see. It's your captain's log in that case."

"Captain's log?" Viviani's interest piqued.

Mr. Hill held it out further. "This is simply where you record your thoughts, Viviani. Your days. It's not supposed to be perfect. It's supposed to be *you*."

"Well, that's good. I'm kinda far from perfect."

Viviani took the book. The cover was smooth brown leather, soft like buttery velvet. It even had a long leather cord to bind it shut. And the pages! Creamy, thick, and *empty*. Viviani's fingers suddenly itched to put her pen nib to this page, to create stories that would sing and dance and kick and tumble and juggle. She'd make this her word playground, a playground safe from name-calling and whispers and hurt.

Her eyes stung. "Are you sure this is for me?"

"It's just an old journal I had lying around." Mr. Hill waved her off. "Don't you worry about that. I can't stand the thought of your stories coming to The End."

Later that night, after everyone was asleep, Viviani snuggled into her covers and brought out the book and her favorite ink pen. She licked the pen and began to write.

Dear

Viviani paused. She didn't like the idea of *Dear Diary*, not one bit. So sappy. But *Dear Captain's Log* sounded silly, too, and all storytellers know the importance of choosing the right word. At last, she decided:

Dear Friend,

My name is Viviani Joffre Fedeler, and I have an antagonist. But here's the thing. She's not a mustache-twirling, head-thrown-back-with-laughter kind of villain like Shere Khan or Dracula. No, this one...well, I'd like her as a friend if she wasn't so darn aggravating! Merit likes photography and she's owned camels and she even has pierced ears! And now, now, I've promised to show her a ghost. How am I supposed to do that, Friend? How will this story end? (Foreshadowing: it doesn't look good....)

Viviani chewed on her pen, leaving ink smudges on her cheeks. What she needed were some good, scary ideas. The writer Geoffrey Crayon leapt to mind. Mr. Crayon was, of course, actually the pen name of Washington Irving, who knew all about chilling things like Rip Van Winkle and the Headless Horseman. He'd created quite a bit of heart-pounding terror with his stories.

She wrote down her favorite quote from him:

I am always at a loss to know how much to believe of my own stories.

Viviani tapped the smooth paper with her pen nib, leaving behind small splashes of ink that looked like spiders. "Me, too, Mr. Crayon. Me, too."

Big Red was *real*, Viv was sure of it. But how would Merit believe it without seeing it? She had to *see* it. Viv kept writing:

HOW TO SEE A GHOST:

—Invent special ghost-seeing glasses.

—Coat it in flour to see it.

—*Summon it with a séance?!*
(No way Eva will do this....)

—*Lure it with candy.*

—<u>*Make one up.*</u>

CHAPTER EIGHTEEN

Stage Presentations,

Dewey Decimal 792.02

SEE ALSO: *theater, juvenile; musicals, juvenile*

Make one up! That's it! It was an aha moment for Viviani. She was *excellent* at making things up. Viviani couldn't guarantee that the real Big Red would show up on the night of the sleepover, but she could give Merit the experience nonetheless.

First things first: The next morning, Viviani ran to Mama, who was wringing laundry through the hand-cranked iron washer. She helped pin three pieces of clothes on the line that hung down the length of their apartment hallway before she asked, "Mama, can I have a sleepover Sunday night?"

"Ah, I knew I wasn't getting your help for nothing,"

Mama said. "Red, you're just *barely* on the other side of the last time you got in trouble."

"But I am on the other side, Mama! I'm free—I made it!" Viviani stretched out her arms, palms up, and her mother laughed.

"It's this girl at school," Viviani continued. "Merit. She's new to America, and I promised I'd show her around the libr—"

"Yes," Viv's mother said, huffing a curl off her forehead. "Of course." If there was one thing Cornelia Fedeler understood, it was coming to America friendless. She'd been that very girl herself years before. Viviani had heard Mama's stories of arriving from Colombia not knowing a soul.

Next, Viv knew she needed help to carry out her plan. She set off in search of reinforcements.

"Please please please, Eva? I don't want to have a sleepover without you."

Eva sighed. "It'll never work. No way."

"Please please please, Edouard? Nobody can come up with a plan like you."

He eventually put down his book and declared, "It'll work, with the right preparation."

"Please please please, John? Nobody knows this library at night like you."

John Jr. grinned. "It'll work, but I'm bringing Carroll, too."

It was decided that they needed a headquarters where they could discuss their plan. So after school, all three Fedeler children plus one reluctant Eva followed Carroll down West Forty-Fourth to his home in the Algonquin Hotel, where his father was head chef. They passed under the green awnings outside and through the double glass doors into the elaborate lobby, stuffed with couches and mirrors and dark wood and tall palm trees in planters. They weaved through the dining area, where one table of guests still sat, despite the empty plates and glasses and dirty napkins that indicated their meal had ended hours before.

"Carroll!" the guests called in unison, jovial and smiling, raising their glasses. One woman with dark bobbed hair, a pearl necklace, and a grin like a blade slice waved them over. "Join us!"

Viviani knew, from events at the library and from Carroll's stories, that this group of people was the Algonquin Round Table, some of America's finest novelists, playwrights, and theater critics. They met here every day to brainstorm, laugh, and talk about art. Normally, Viviani would leap at a chance to be so close to such famous storytellers. But today, she was on a mission to craft her own story.

Carroll waved. "Can't today, Mrs. Parker. My friends and I are working on a project. For, uh, school."

"See there, Dorothy," one man said, laying a hand on Mrs. Parker's shoulder. "You're so far gone, innocence won't even rub elbows with you." The woman playfully shoved the fellow while the rest of the table howled with laughter.

Carroll laughed and kept walking. As Viv turned to follow, she heard the woman pick up the previous conversation: "As I was saying, ridicule may be a shield, but it is not a weapon."

"It is in a schoolyard," Viviani said, before her brain could stop her. If she hadn't been stabbed by Merit's accusation, she doubted she'd be here, cooking up an elaborate scheme to produce a ghost.

Dorothy Parker's eyes shone. "Touché! All the niceties of society disappear in a schoolyard. Here's to you surviving that barbarism, kids. Total anarchy." She raised a glass to toast Viviani, who smiled and tipped her own imaginary glass.

The group swung through the huge kitchen on their route through the hotel and waved hello to Carroll's father. Carroll plucked a tray of petit fours from a tabletop, spun, and swooped up a tray of tiny biscuits topped with salmon, cream cheese, and chives.

John Jr.'s eyes widened. "Nobody has better snacks than Carroll."

They swung through doors on the other side of the kitchen, down a narrow back hallway, and into a meeting room. It was windowless and quiet, with a massive mahogany table and loads of spinning, wheeled chairs. It was the perfect place to hatch their plan. This would be a production of sorts, just like the playwright Edna Ferber, outside right now at that lunch table, might create. At least, that's what Viviani told herself.

Viviani opened her captain's log to her plan and smoothed the page:

CREATING A GHOST:

—Practice spooky moans

—Come up with a disguise—red beard?!
Sheet? COVERALLS!

—Find a hammer

—Get a flashlight

—Smoke—maybe from cigarettes?
(Eva crossed that one off right away.)

—Smoke—maybe from cigarettes?

—Remember to turn down furnace that afternoon so it's
COLD! BRRRRRR!

Viviani had also drawn a map of the basement, which was the creepiest place in the library and where they had last seen the ghost. It also helped that it was the spot farthest away from where her parents might be.

As soon as Viviani shared her ideas, John Jr. took charge. He grabbed the list and scrawled *firecrackers!* at the bottom, which Viviani promptly crossed out. "Are you a complete knucklehead?"

"Aw shucks, Red. I'd never actually do it. But, boy, have I ever wanted to. Can you imagine the bang in that big, hollow space?"

He and Carroll shared a devious look.

"Slap me some skin," Carroll said, just like Al Jolson did in his movies. John Jr. slid his palm over Carroll's.

John Jr. then gave everyone a role, told them where they were supposed to be and when, what to say and what to wear—he was a real pro.

"It's almost like you've tricked someone like this before, John," said Edouard, his eyes narrowing.

John winked and pretended to twirl a mustache. "Leave it to me. We'll give Merit a bit of a scare. Nothing wrong with a harmless little trick."

"Not a trick!" Viviani said quickly, spinning in her meeting-room chair. "Eva won't play along if it's tricking."

Eva nodded vigorously and shot a look at the rest of the group.

"It's not tricking—" Viviani searched for the right word. "It's—"

"Duping." Carroll grinned.

"Fooling!" John Jr. added.

"Conning," Edouard said.

"Performing!" Viviani said. "Just like a play."

But Viviani was too late. Eva was already gathering her schoolbag and headed out the door.

"It's not nice, whatever name you call it." Eva looked at Viviani with shining eyes. "Viv, count me out. You're going to have to do this one without me."

CHAPTER NINETEEN

Carousels,
Dewey Decimal 745.592

SEE ALSO: *merry-go-rounds, amusement parks*

Dear Friend,

Never in all my cockamamie ideas has Eva said, "Do this without me." I've never done anything without her by my side. We're not tricking Merit; we're just opening her world—how sad, to dismiss all stories as lies. Merit sees everything as stacks of atoms and molecules, something you can capture in a photograph. I see the world as stacks of words and stories, something that can never fully be captured. Not everything has to be proved to be believed! I can understand why her

world works that way. It makes sense—it's orderly
and organized. But why can't she understand my
world, too?

The following day after school, instead of walking
home, Viviani was determined to make Eva smile.
Their last conversation at the hotel had been as uncom-
fortable as sand in swim clothes, and Viv wanted Eva to
see the sunshine of the situation instead. She tugged
Eva to the trolley stop at Third and Forty-Second.
"Come on," she said. "We're officially on winter break!
Let's go to Central Park and celebrate."

The trolley clanged to a stop in front of them, its
metal wheels screeching on the tracks embedded in the
road. The trolley was a box on wheels, essentially, with
wide, low windows. It was propelled by swaying, zippy
electrical lines overhead. Viv and Eva hauled themselves up the metal stairs. Viv dropped two nickels into
the box near the trolley driver, and he swung the iron
cage door shut behind them with the huge lever at
his side. The streetcar moved slowly, humans and
automobiles dashing ahead, New York City propelled
by a zippiness all its own.

The air was cold and crisp, but the sun was shining,

and Viviani and Eva clung to the trolley with one hand, hanging off the back side, casting long, wintry shadows on the street. Viviani stretched farther and farther out over the tracks, hanging on with just one hand.

"Viv, stop!" Eva said.

Viviani grinned at her. "Can't. I'm training to grab the brass ring." It was rather like saying, *I'm training for the Boston Marathon* or *I'm training to spend all the money my rich, estranged uncle will bequeath me when he dies.* Sure, those things sometimes happen to regular people, but c'mon! The brass ring! It was part of a carousel game, and it was small, not even as big as a bracelet, and hung off a metal arm jutting from a pole. Carousel riders on the outer horses tried to grab the ring while spinning past, and it was always, *always* juuuuuust out of reach.

"Yeah, okay," Eva said, rolling her eyes. "Nobody grabs the brass ring. My dad says he thinks it's nailed on its hook."

The trolley jerked, clanged its bell, and followed the tracks and wires all the way up to Columbus Circle. There, Viv and Eva hopped off before the trolley had completely stopped, much to the driver's dismay.

Central Park looked magical in winter: the bare tree limbs draped themselves in shimmery ice crystals, the snow piled like puffy clouds around trunks and rocks and statues. Viv and Eva wandered past the reservoir and the sheep meadow. ("Baaaaa!" shouted Viviani; "Baaaaa!" answered a sheep.) Past Umpire Rock and the sand garden, over and *swish!* down a spiral slide on the playground, and around the casino that John Jr. called a "whoopee joint." They made their way to the carousel.

"Come on," Viv said, grabbing her best friend's hand. "Let's go. My treat."

Viviani picked a purple stallion with a pink mane, rearing up on two legs. Because it had stopped high up on its pole, Viviani had to scramble to mount the horse. The silly drop-waist dresses her mama insisted she wear ("So stylish!") made all climbing—carousel horses, trees, flagpoles, bookstacks—that much more difficult. Eva picked a sensible cream-colored horse with flowers in its mane.

The calliope music twanged from the center of the carousel, and the horses lurched forward. "Once upon a time," Viviani began. Eva smiled, for even if she didn't care for Viv's pranks, she did indeed love Viv's stories.

"Once upon a time, there was a brilliant team of circus performers. Viviani the Magnificent . . ." She paused to gesture at herself, then swept her hand to Eva. "And Amazing Eva, the Horse Whisperer."

Eva sat up straighter.

"These two performers were the stars of the Big

Top, adored by fans nationwide. But then . . . tragedy struck!" Viviani pretended to tumble off her horse. The whole merry-go-round wobbled.

"My leg!" she wailed, gripping her knee. "However will I perform again?"

The carousel operator was not amused. "Hey, hey, hey! Take a seat, kid!" he said in a thick Brooklyn accent. He jabbed the end of his lit cigar at Viviani.

"I shall never ride again!" Viviani cried dramatically. She stood and began walking against the spin of the carousel, ducking and weaving through the bobbing horses, across the wooden planks of the ride. The carousel swayed with her steps, and Viviani garnered scowls and frowns from the other riders. Eva laughed and clutched the brass pole that held her horse.

"I said, get on a horse, kid!" the operator yelled.

Viviani grinned and climbed aboard a horse just in front of Eva, on the outer edge of the carousel. She leaned back, shouting the story over her shoulder: "The circus went broke because one half of their star equestrian team had been so gravely injured. Hundreds of clowns and acrobats and performers out of a job! But worst of all, Amazing Eva needed to keep working, so she joined a different circus."

"Amazing Eva wouldn't do that. She wouldn't leave Viviani the Magnificent," Eva protested.

"She would if she needed to feed her beloved hungry horses." Viviani smiled back at her friend. Eva considered this and hugged the neck of her carousel horse.

"So Viviani the Magnificent trained and trained and trained and became more magnificent than ever. Magnificenter."

"That's not a word."

"It is now."

Eva cocked an eyebrow at her.

Viv said, "Words get made up all the time, Eva! How else do you think they get created?"

Eva shrugged.

Viviani stood up on her horse slowly, carefully. She placed one foot atop her horse, the other on a different horse, so that she was straddling two ponies bobbing at different times. Eva gasped and giggled.

"Introducing Viviani the Magnificenter!" Viviani cried, flinging her arms open.

"KID, DON'T MAKE ME STOP THIS RIDE!"

Viviani slid back down to her original horse, just as the gleaming brass ring came into view. She leaned far, far to the right, practically riding the ribs of the pony. She clung to the brass pole of the horse with just the tippy-tippy top of her fingertips, as she had done off the back of the trolley. Viv angled herself and grabbed the prize brass ring off the hook as they circled by.

Eva squealed and clapped. The brass ring! She did it! Viviani would get a free repeat ride thanks to that little gem.

Viviani turned back to Eva. "And when she snagged the top prize, the Golden Ring, Viviani the Magnificenter gave the valuable prize to the Big Top Circus so they could sell it and stay in business. She and her best friend could keep performing together. Forever."

Eva beamed. Grabbing the brass ring off the carousel was rare enough, but Viviani's storytelling made it downright magical. Viviani tried to hand the brass ring back to Eva, but it slipped from her grip, and *flip!* It slid right underneath the carousel.

"The ring!" Eva wailed. "Our circus will go bust without it! Our friendship ruined!"

The carousel horses slowed, and the spinning and the music stopped. Eva scrambled off her horse and grabbed Viviani's hand. "Let's go find that ring!"

Eva and Viviani fought their way through the thorny bushes and scrubby weeds lining the side of the carousel. Viviani smiled.

"Admit it, Eva: you felt like a real circus performer back there. Sometimes stories *feel* true. Even if they're nonsense, they aren't lies. Not really."

Eva paused.

"When the feelings are real, the stories are real.

Help me show Merit a ghost, Eva. I truly think she *wants* to see a ghost. She wants a photograph of one."

Eva looked up at the carousel tottering nearby, almost overhead. "But, Viv, it's still just a story. Those are still just fake horses trotting in a silly circle."

At that moment, the carousel operator stomped his foot on the wooden platform above. The music started up, and the carousel horses slowly began to spin and bob.

Viviani grinned and pointed underneath the merry-go-round. There, in the shadows below the wooden slats of the ride, was a real horse and a real donkey. The pair marched in a dusty circle, shafts of sunlight streaking through from above. The bits in their mouths were attached to the underside of the ride, driving the carousel.

"See, Eva?" Viviani said. "That's real horsepower. Real donkeys and horses down *here* make the fake horses up *there* trot."

Viv scooped up Eva's hands.

"Every story is true underneath it all."

CHAPTER TWENTY

Haunted Places,

Dewey Decimal 133.12

SEE ALSO: *ghosts—United States; apparitions*

"So Edouard will stand here . . . ," Viviani muttered to herself. She stood in the windowless stairwell, on the landing one floor down from their apartment. From this perch, she could see into the basement one floor below. "Yes, that'll work."

Once Eva had agreed to help, the plan had gone full steam ahead. Now Viviani was mapping everything out one last time before Merit's arrival tomorrow.

Viviani took several more steps down into the basement, down the cold, red tile stairs, toward Mr. Green's custodial closet at the bottom. The one that was always locked. The one that had only a single key. The graveyard of bones.

This was the part of the basement where she was not allowed to go.

She shivered.

Drip, drip, drip.

The brass handrail suddenly turned ice cold beneath her touch. She jerked her hand back.

The lights overhead flickered. They always did that, though. Didn't they?

The furnace whooshed up the stairs, sending a blast of heat, drying out her eyes.

The air around Viviani chilled suddenly. Did she imagine that?

Crrrreeeeeeaaaaakkkkk!

Below, the custodial closet door eased open. *On its own?* No, wait.

Mr. Green slid out, silent as a ghost. From where she was above, Viviani could see a small balding spot on the top of his head. Mr. Green turned and locked the door behind him with his special key, the only key to his terrible closet.

Viviani felt nauseated. She thought she might faint. What a terrible place to pass out, so close to *the* closet where her skin could be stripped from her very bones!

Mr. Green didn't see her, though. He turned and ran his fingers over the letters of the sign hanging on the door.

"Terry Green," he whispered as he did. Terry? That was his first name? He nodded once. "Terry Green."

He picked up his bucket and mop and lumbered down the hallway.

Viviani leaned as far as she could over the railing to glance at the door. It had once been painted black, but it was now peeling from the humidity in that drippy moist basement.

The sign didn't say *Terry Green* at all. It read *Custodial Closet*.

Dear Friend,

Mama says imagination has wings. Like John Jr.'s pigeons. And most of the time I agree—it feels like I'm flying when I'm reading and telling stories. Swooping through the sky, bouncing on clouds. All feathers and wind and whoosh.

But I sometimes feel like imagination is the birdcage instead. Once I imagine something—like a ghost—it's hard for my brain to break free and see things any other way.

I hope this plan works.

Oh, and speaking of plans, this was John Jr.'s latest: the library is fully decorated for the holidays—poinsettias, menorahs, a tree covered in shiny foil ribbons—all so pretty! And today, Santa was in the children's room for story time. John Jr. paid Edouard a quarter to sit on Santa's lap with a Boy Scout flask—open!—in his pocket. Ed sat, the water inside spilled out, and that poor Santa thought "the young tyke" had an accident all over him! When the flask was discovered, boy, were those librarians mad—at John Jr.! Edouard of course managed to convince them all that he never knew John Jr. had slipped the flask into his pocket.

All this to say: I can't imagine how my plan could fail with these two hooligans on my side.

CHAPTER TWENTY-ONE

Secrets,

Dewey Decimal 155.4

SEE ALSO: *mysteries, riddles*

It's unfortunate that *stone* has become associated with *unfeeling*: "heart of stone" and "cold as stone." Secrets seep deep into stone, and there they stay; Leo Lenox the library lion was no exception. He was a top-notch secret keeper. Folks told him all sorts of secrets, confidences from people who visited the library from all over the world:

"I cheated on my math test."

"I'm scared to ask her for a date."

"My family doesn't know I'm in New York."

Viviani often sprawled across Lenox's back, hugging his neck, telling him stories and small secrets. She'd climb atop the small wall to his left and drape herself over him. Today, she whispered:

"Merit will be here in five minutes. I'm so nervous. Lenox, lend me some of your courage, will you? I just don't want to be called a liar."

Were Lenox able to speak, he'd likely remind Viviani that courage is simply fear stuffed with hope. But she'd likely not hear it at this moment, even if he could share his thoughts on the matter. Nervous people make poor listeners.

Behind Viviani, the Doughnut Sisters were back yet again, peddling for-charity wares by telling library visitors that "those stamps inside are a—" "—tragedy of society." "So wasteful that a person—" "—would spend that much money on buying stamps." "Buy doughnuts instead." And behind *them*, a group of kids from a choir were gathered on the wide library steps, singing hymns and carols from prim and proper songbooks. Their choir director flicked her wrists and twiddled her fingers, and the kids' choir robes swung while their songs lifted into the cold New York sky in puffs.

"There she is!" Eva yelled from the back of Leo Astor. Viviani and Eva hopped off their respective lions and scrambled down the steps.

Merit approached with her father, her camera

swinging about her neck. Her father handed Papa an overnight bag, and the two began to chat. Merit blinked at the Doughnut Sisters, the choir.

"There are people fund-raising. And singing," she said. The children's choir started the "Hallelujah" chorus while the Doughnut Sisters brandished their pastries at visitors.

"That? Oh, there's always something like that going on here." Viviani realized that even though she'd heard the choir singing while she'd been chatting with Lenox, she hadn't actually *listened* to them. They were quite good. And the church bells surrounding the library were coordinated with their song—it was downright magical.

Merit grinned. She pulled her camera to her eye, squinted into the eyepiece, and snapped a photograph. "It's just—well, not everyone has a choir singing in front of their house, Viviani."

Viviani blinked, then grinned as Eva and Merit shared a smile. "I guess not."

The choir director, a behemoth of a woman in a massive fur coat with the fox head still attached to the collar, approached them. She shoved a pamphlet into each of their hands.

"We're always looking for new talent, girls."

Merit smiled at her. "Your choir is very good."

"Yes, it is," the furry woman sniffed. "And the city needs it. The *children* need it. I always say: fill the air with lovely children's voices. So innocent! So beautiful and harmonious! Replace the sound of that vulgar jazzy noise."

"Jazz music?" Viviani asked. "Oh, my mother loves jazz!"

The woman looked down her nose at Viviani, and from Viv's point of view, it appeared as though the fox fur lolling about her neck was doing the same. Two sets of beady, judging eyes. She heard Merit snap a photo of this interaction.

"Well, then," the woman said. "You are a lost cause."

Viviani grinned. "Oh, you're not the first to tell me that. The librarians have been saying it for years."

The trio of girls burst into laughter. Viviani thought this sleepover might just turn out okay after all. They went back to the fathers to get Merit's bag.

"Let's go, then," Merit said, folding the camera back inside its box. "Let's see this ghost."

Viviani gulped down a quick-rising bubble of fear. "We can't go right now," she stammered. "We, uh, we have to wait until the dead of night. It's actually pretty scary."

Merit's eye roll spoke volumes. "Viviani, nothing can scare me."

Papa turned toward the girls at that, clapping a hand over Merit's shoulder. "Nothing, huh? 'Though she be but little, she is fierce!' I do believe my own fearless daughter may have just met her match!"

Fearless? Viviani glanced back at Lenox in a last silent plea: *Oh, Lenox, lend me some of your courage, will you?*

A sleepover in the library is no ordinary sleepover. That goes without saying, but there it is nonetheless. First, the three girls raced elevators; then they pitted the elevators versus the stairs. They played telephone in the wooden phone booths: "Hello? Yes! President Coolidge on the line for you, Miss Mubarak." They pushed one another on wheeled book carts, suppressing their squeals as much as possible so they wouldn't get caught. Luckily, the damage they did ramming one into a doorframe was minimal, thanks to the brass edgings placed there to prevent just such nicks in the marble. Although it's likely the architects of this fine building never foresaw three girls freewheeling about on a book cart during a sleepover.

They snuck into the stacks and climbed up the heavy iron bookshelves, fancying themselves scaling Mount Kilimanjaro. Merit pointed to the tip-top of the stacks and shouted, "To the summit, friends!" Viviani smiled down at Eva, then over at Merit, and thought, *With an imagination like hers, everything will be all right. Maybe. I think.*

And all the while, all the while, Merit took photographs. Careful, meticulous photographs.

"Can I see the Inverted Jenny?" Merit asked, snapping the camera closed.

"Absolutely! Follow me!" Viviani took off at a full sprint, the other two scrambling behind her.

When they got to the Stuart Room, they crept in silently. A soft glow illuminated the room, thanks to the dusky sky melting through the skylight. It seemed to Viviani that a single beam of sunlight shone down on the case that held the Inverted Jenny. It was almost closing time, so most of the patrons were gone.

Except for one. Mr. Hill was there, as usual. "Hello, Viviani. Hello, Viviani's friends!"

Viviani smiled. "Hi, Mr. Hill." She started to tell him that she'd been writing in her captain's log, but stopped. Suddenly that seemed like something she wanted to keep to herself.

"Wow," Merit breathed, circling the case, studying the stamp. "It really is upside down."

Viviani could see the admiration deep in Merit's eyes. "It really is."

Merit snapped a photograph of the stamp while Viviani, Eva, and Mr. Hill looked on.

A long, low, teeth-rattling gong sounded. The noise resembled a tumbling, roiling thundercloud. "That's us," Viviani said, dashing for the door. "Come on."

The confusion on Merit's face made her laugh.

"My mom rings a gong when it's dinnertime," Viviani said. "The building is too big for a bell."

Merit shook her head and suppressed a grin. "A gong for a dinner bell in a library. Now I've seen it all."

Viviani beamed. This girl, this mysterious, brave, stubborn girl who came from the other side of the world, had seen it all *here*, in Viv's home, in the library.

But then Merit slid to a stop. She whirled about. "I take that back. I *haven't* yet seen it all. One ghost to go."

Another low, ominous gong sounded. Viviani felt it in her very bones.

CHAPTER TWENTY-TWO

Clocks,

Dewey Decimal 749.3

SEE ALSO: *timepieces, watches, chronometers*

In the Main Reading Room, there is a clock embedded in the fine, scrolling woodwork above the librarian's desk. If you're inclined to those noisy, showy, cuckooing clocks, you won't find them here, for this one does not *bing* or *bong*, as this is a library clock. Instead, the seconds whisk softly away like page turns.

So at the stroke of midnight, when the hands aligned at the top of the clock in the pale slant of moonlight, they did so in silence. Like the whisper of a passing black cat or the sigh of a ghost. Midnight is far creepier when it arrives in this way: a new day slicing in to cut away the last, the passing of yesterday, and the fragile first moments of a new day taking shaky, unsure steps.

Viviani eased the heavy oak door of their eight-room apartment shut behind their group of three, and the small *click* of the brass doorknob echoed in the cavernous, cold library like a bone snapping. Eva jumped. Goose bumps raced up the arms of the girls as they slid in slippered feet across the wide marble expanses, the chill of the floor seeping into their soles and increasing their shivers. It was like walking through a tomb.

Viviani hid a grin. Technically, she didn't *need* to bring Merit and Eva through the reading room to get to the basement from their apartment; in fact, it was quite out of the way—akin to two city blocks. But there was nothing like it to set the mood.

The Main Reading Room was filled with hundreds of tables, chairs, and dimmed brass lamps. On every inch of wall surrounding the huge open space stood shelves of books and books and books, two stories high. The creeping shadows, coupled with the silent, dark stacks of leather-bound spines, looked to Viviani like the ribs of a skeleton beneath a massive sleeping beast.

Plus, well, Viviani knew they couldn't head to the basement at exactly midnight. Mr. Eames, the night guard, would be there now, keys jangling, lips whistling, bow tie bowing. In another eight minutes, he'd move on.

"Here is where it happened," Viviani whispered into

the massive dark room, and her words were whisked into a space as big as a football field. "Here is where Big Red died. While working on the ceiling."

The three girls looked up, up, up—five stories high, to the creation suspended above them. "It's so high I'm dizzy just looking at it," Eva whispered.

Merit stopped in the middle of the reading room and turned slowly, slowly. "Wow," she breathed, and the cold, cavernous space made her breath wisp. "Look at all this stuff I don't know yet."

Viviani smiled at the *yet* part. Her father always said bold learners think in terms of *yet*.

The sixteen two-story windows were the only source of light, and the moonbeams that snuck in were weak. When a cloud passed over the sliver of moon, it caused shadows to crawl over the stacks of books, making the books appear as if they were alive. Waking. Breathing. Squirming.

Viviani knew just how alive those bookcases truly were. At least in her heart they were; the stories they held felt real and teeming with life. "Come on," she whispered, heading for the wide, smooth stairs. "Big Red lives in the basement."

When they reached the stairs, Merit didn't hesitate: she slung one leg over the sleek wooden banister and swooshed down the stairs to the story below, nightgown billowing, camera around her neck swaying. Viviani pinched back another grin and followed suit. The cool banister, the whooshing air around her: Viviani's goose bumps got goose bumps.

Eva shook her head. "You two are going to break your necks." She padded down the flight of stairs to catch up.

On the first floor, they heard it: whistling!

Viviani grabbed the hands of her friends and pulled them into a nook just under the grand staircase.

"The ghost?" Eva asked, eyes wide.

Viviani shook her head. "Worse," she whispered. "Mr. Eames."

The night guard would not only deduct five points from Viviani's Master Thief score but also send them straight back to the apartment at this time of night. Everyone at Viviani's school wanted to see a picture of this ghost now. She couldn't get turned back at this point by Mr. Eames. Too much was riding on this.

Sure enough, Mr. Eames clattered and jangled up the stairs. He turned the corner and paused, two feet away from the trio of girls lurking in the shadows nearby.

Eva squeezed Viviani's hand. Merit bit her bottom lip.

Mr. Eames sneezed. It sounded in the dark, cavernous space like a gunshot, and Eva whimpered.

"God bless me," he said with a chuckle. He straightened his bow tie, and on he went.

Viviani exhaled. Good thing Mr. Eames was as loud as a herd of cattle. The trio crept from their hiding spot.

They wound deeper and deeper into the library, leaving the windows, and most of the light, behind. They finally reached the basement and headed down the corridor to the stacks, past the rooms where Viviani wasn't allowed. Soon, there was little more than the small, sweeping yellow beam from the crusty Ray-O-Vac flashlight Viviani had snatched from her father's toolbox. The girls gripped one another's cold, clammy hands and felt their way through the darkness toward the boiler room. Viviani's heart drummed inside her rib cage; even though she knew the plan, she couldn't help but think of the *actual* red-whiskered ghost and *his* plans. For all her scheming, Viviani didn't have a plan for what to do if Big Red really appeared!

CLANG. The radiator kicked on with an immense noise.

"The hammer!" Merit yelped. Viviani knew it was the radiator, but it sure did sound like a ghost's hammer. She had to admit to being very pleased with this timing: Merit wanted to see a ghost, and Viviani would give her one.

Then:

Whoosh.

Mumble.

Thump!

"Shhhh!" Eva said, clasping Viviani's hand. "Did you hear that?"

The flashlight flickered out.

Merit gasped at the sudden complete darkness. Viviani whacked the flashlight with the palm of her hand, and the light sputtered back to life.

Swoosh.

Thu–thump.

CRASH!

Eva squeaked. Merit and Viviani practically jumped out of their slippers. Eva turned and started skidding and sliding back toward the stairs. Viviani grabbed her arm, which made Eva jolt. Viv held the flashlight under her chin; lit from below, she looked like a goblin. Viviani winked at her, reassuring her *It's all part of the plan, remember?* Eva nodded back shakily.

Suddenly, a figure scrabbled out from behind one of the massive seven-tiered shelves. A figure wearing bulky clothes, a flat woolen cap, and *red whiskers!* Carrying *a hammer!*

The flashlight clicked off. Darkness swallowed the girls.

Merit screamed. It was a true wailer: a deep, hollow, smothered-by-blackness scream, muffled by books and maps and rows upon rows of thick iron bookcases.

A flash popped. Merit's camera blinded them.

Viviani blinked back the dots swimming in her vision and grinned to beat all. The plan was working! She turned the flashlight back on. The beam found the red-whiskered face, whose eyes were wild, terrified. The Fedelers were putting on quite the show!

But then—*what*? The figure ripped the red beard off, revealing John Jr.'s bewildered face. Carroll Case scrambled out from behind the shelves, too, knocking several books off the stack as he rounded the corner. John Jr. and Carroll stood wide-eyed, hands on knees, chests heaving in front of the three girls.

Viviani thrust her fist on her hip. "John!" she hissed. "This is not part of the plan!"

John shook his head, his eyes growing wider, wilder. The lump in his throat bobbed.

"Viv!" John shout-whispered. "That crash wasn't us."

Thoughts swirled through Viviani's brain:

Our plan is dead.

The crash wasn't you?

Why . . . what . . . WHO?

BIG RED!

Viviani's eyes locked with John's, and they grew

rounder, more fierce, and her stomach lurched. Sometimes seconds can feel like hours; instead of whisking by like page turns, they thump heavily like a book dropped on a toe.

"Then . . . who was it?"

"Uggghhhhhhmmmmmm!"

The five kids heard it again: a deep moan, a guttural groan, wailing from behind the broken pieces of furniture near Papa's workshop.

Viviani remembered her papa's words about Big Red: *Killed by his own mischief. And now he seeks to destroy it whenever it is near.* If this wasn't mischief, Viviani didn't know what was.

Thump!

"AhhhOOOOOO!"

The flashlight flickered off.

Viviani smacked it back on and swept the beam across the faces of her comrades. Their terrified expressions all said the same thing, so at last Viviani shouted it:

"RUN!"

CHAPTER TWENTY-THREE

Pranks,

Dewey Decimal 818.607

SEE ALSO: *tomfooleries, monkeyshines, practical jokes*

The five kids huffed and puffed and slid and scrambled up a flight of cold stairs.

"Edouard!" John Jr. hissed at the first landing. "Abort mission! Abort!"

They clambered up another half flight. On the last curve of the stairwell, they rounded the corner and *umph!*

Viviani, in the lead, ran smack into the chest of something tall and dark and smelling like quite a bit of pipe smoke. She yalped.

Mr. Green lifted a lantern, and the jumping flame inside it threw skipping shadows over his scowling face. Of course he'd use something creepy and old-fashioned like a lantern! He bent over the kids. Was he *drooling*? Viviani pictured him clutching a knife and fork instead of a lantern and a broom. She stepped backward and nearly tumbled down the stairs.

"What are you doing?" he growled.

"Mr. Green," Viviani gasped. Honestly, how could no one *ever* hear him coming? "The . . . the *ghost*. We heard it!"

"There ain't no ghost round here! If I find you kids have broken anything, I'll—" He stopped there, pinching his lips tight, but Viviani filled in the rest: *boil you up in a nice broth.* She shivered.

Edouard skidded around the corner just then, looking from the group of kids to Mr. Green. His role in the plan had been to follow the girls down the basement stairs, dropping items and brushing things against them when the flashlight "flickered." The look on his face screamed, *What happened?*

"Go on!" Mr. Green yelled at them, and pointed up the last half flight of stairs to the apartment door. "Git!"

The six kids scrambled to the door. They swung it wide, ducked inside, and slammed it shut, backs leaning against it, panting.

"VIVIANI JOFFRE FEDELER!"

Mama stood in the living room in a familiar livid

stance: arms crossed, toes tapping. She wore a thin pink robe, and the rags in her hair (tied there to achieve perfect pin curls) stood out all over her head like Medusa's snakes. Viviani wasn't sure what was scarier: her mad mother or the wailing ghost in the basement.

But Mama's glare softened when she saw the terror in the kids' eyes. "Is everything all right? What on earth happened?"

Viviani gulped. "Mama, we heard it! We heard the red-whiskered ghost! We heard Big Red!" Her heart flip-flopped just thinking of the unexplained moan they heard.

Mama's gaze slid to John Jr., who shrugged. "I don't know what we heard, Mama. It was probably just . . . a creaky floorboard or something." Carroll nodded a little too enthusiastically.

"That's not true and you know it, John." Viviani glared at them, and John Jr. sheepishly avoided her gaze. Did he not want to get in trouble? Or was he embarrassed by how terrified he'd been just moments before? Either way, he was leaving Viviani stranded with her story.

Mama's shoulders fell. "John. Carroll. Edouard. Off to bed. Now." She pointed a well-manicured fingernail at John and Edouard's shared room.

"Viviani, you too. Take your guests into your room. I'll deal with you all tomorrow."

She spun on her heel and went into her room.

Viviani, Merit, and Eva trudged to Viviani's room. Merit slammed the door.

"You tried to trick me."

Viviani looked down. "No. Well, yes, kinda. But the ghost *is* real! We just can't summon him on command. You seemed like you needed to believe in a story, that you *needed* to see a ghost, so—"

"You *are* a liar, Viviani Joffre Fedeler. The others tried to tell me that you just like to have some fun and make up stories, but now I see it. Now I know."

Viviani felt sick. "No, you don't understand! We were just playing a little prank."

Viviani looked at Eva, who lowered her gaze to her slippers. She'd be no help. "Merit, I'll admit that we tried to scare you, but I didn't lie about Big Red. Don't you see? That noise—it couldn't have been John Jr. or Carroll or Edouard! They were standing right there with us when we heard that moan!"

Eva rubbed her arms and nodded.

"Merit," Viviani said, "there's really a ghost down there!"

Merit's lips tightened, but her eyes swam with tears.

A drop slid down her cheek, and she wiped it away furiously with a balled fist. "I thought we were starting to be friends, Viviani. I was really beginning to like you. But I don't want to be friends with someone who thinks it's funny to trick me or scare me. You wanted me to look like a fool."

Merit crawled into her sleeping pallet on the floor and turned her back toward Eva and Viv. Eva silently turned off the light without meeting Viviani's gaze and got into her own pallet without even saying good night.

Viviani flopped and flipped in the dark, watching the plaster ceiling in her room grow from black to gray to pale yellow. How could she sleep knowing her home was haunted?

She grabbed her captain's log and scrawled inside:

Dear Friend,

> *Merit hates me and I don't blame her.*
> *Eva is mad at me and I don't blame her.*

She tapped her pencil against her teeth. Her stomach twisted as she wrote:

> *If it wasn't John Jr., who—or WHAT—is in*
> *the basement?*

CHAPTER TWENTY-FOUR

Chores,

Dewey Decimal 331

SEE ALSO: *jobs, responsibilities, work*

The next morning, both of Viviani's guests left the sleepover early, which only happens when the sleepover was a disaster. Viviani yelled goodbye, one hand on Lenox's stony mane, one hand waving furiously, in an effort to get even one of them to look her in the eye.

Neither Merit nor Eva looked back.

Viviani sighed and laid her forehead against the cool stone lion. "I've done it now, Lenox." She stayed like that for a long while, until her papa cast a shadow over them both. He laid a strong, firm hand on her shoulder.

"Let's go, Viviani. You're going to help me open up the library today. More chores as punishment for gallivanting around the library at night. Think of it as an opportunity to make up for scaring five years off your mother's life."

Normally, Viviani adored going on rounds with her father. But framed yet again under the guise of "punishment," it suddenly took on a dreaded, ominous role. And so she groaned. "Can we move, Papa?"

Papa ruffled her hair. "Absolutely not. Look, I searched the basement this morning and found nothing. Red, let me share a thought from Mark Twain with you: *You can't depend on your eyes when your imagination is out of focus.* Sound familiar?"

Viviani's shoulders slumped. The last thing she needed was a lecture on imagination.

Papa waggled his eyebrows and handed her his heavy, clattering toolbox. "Nothing, huh? Well, silence is a true friend who never betrays. Follow me."

As they entered the library, they passed Edouard and John Jr., who had apparently been doled out their punishments, based on the mops and buckets they carried.

"Fact," Edouard said drily. "There are approximately one million children between the ages of ten and fifteen employed in the United States currently." He looked at Viviani, holding her father's toolbox. "Now it appears there are one million and three."

"Oh, you and your *facts*, Edouard!" Viviani huffed.

"Have a little imagination, will you? You weren't even there! You didn't hear Big Red! Tell him, Junior, tell him about the ghost! It wasn't creaky floorboards and you know it."

John Jr. shrugged, and the bucket of dirty mop water sloshed. Last night, he'd looked terrified. Today, he looked embarrassed. "We heard something, yes. But a ghost? Honestly, Red, next time? Leave us out of your crazy plans, okay?"

"Please don't call me that anymore. And you wanted to be a part of these plans!"

"Fact," Edouard said. "*You* asked us. We helped."

Edouard and John Jr. dragged their supplies toward the administrative offices up on the second floor. Papa put a hand on Viviani's shoulder. "C'mon, Red."

For the first time ever, Viviani was really beginning to dislike her nickname. Who shares a name with a ghost? "Could you *please* stop calling me that? It's so stupid!" She immediately regretted the outburst, as one usually does with outbursts.

But Papa just scratched his chin. "Sure thing, Firecracker."

First, Viviani held the ladder while Papa twisted lightbulbs into sockets and twisted sentences into stories. "Did I ever tell you that Thomas Edison called two of his kids Dot and Dash, like Morse code?"

Viviani rolled her eyes. "About a million times."

"Yeah? Well, did I tell you that they could talk to each other using just clicks of their tongue, in code?"

Viviani perked up, nearly toppling her father. "Is that true?"

"It could be." Papa shot a single arched eyebrow bouncing down the rungs of the ladder.

Viviani sighed. She was quite tired of *coulds*.

Next chore: oiling the card catalog drawers. The oil smelled earthy, dank, and the oilcan thumped loudly when it was pumped, but Papa didn't care. He was the only one allowed to make noise around here, free from librarian shushes. Fixing things means you get to make all the noise you want.

Papa squirted a drop of oil between his thumb and forefinger and considered it thoughtfully. "Hmmph. Just like squid ink. Did I ever tell you about the time that I wrestled a giant squid?"

Viviani tried very, very hard not to smile since she was being punished, and one must look as miserable as possible while being punished. That was an unspoken rule of being punished. "You did not."

"Oh yes, the squid pulled a shipmate of mine right off the deck of our boat with one of his giant suckers— *shhhhlllllPOP!*—so I pushed up my shirtsleeves and dove in after him."

"That didn't happen."

"It did. I wasn't afraid, you know. You recall I was a sea diver in the navy. *Glub, glub, glub,* all the way to the ocean floor to pick up metal, rifles—all sorts of junk that sank after shipwrecks. So diving in after that monster? Why, I didn't think twice.

"I wrestled that squid underwater, gulping sea and throwing punches, until I finally beat him at his own game."

"Yeah?" Viviani asked despite herself.

"Yes, ma'am. He puffed up large, *up, up, up* like a balloon, and I could tell he was about to propel a huge cloud of poisonous ink my way, so instead, I covered up his blowhole with my very own lips—"

"You put your lips on a giant poisonous squid." Viviani placed her fist on her hip. "Don't squid have multiple blowholes, anyways?"

"Now, listen up, Firecracker. I covered up his blowhole, and when I saw he was about to explode with ink, I blew with all my might, like he was a big ol' trombone. You know what happened next?"

"What?" Viviani couldn't resist asking.

"He imploded!" Papa said, in an *of course* tone of voice. Viviani giggled.

"Nearly died that day, I did. I couldn't see anything in that inky water. Only found my way to the surface by following the bubbles of air up. But I lived to tell the tale."

They moved to the next task: nailing down loose floorboards. Viviani was lost in thought as Papa stepped on the floorboards and they creaked, moaned. She had to admit they did sound ghostly.

"Papa," Viviani said slowly, toting his heavy toolbox.

"Yeah?"

"What's the difference between a storyteller and a liar?"

Papa laughed at first, then realized his daughter was serious. "That's a good question. Did you know that used to be, long, long ago, the words *history* and *story* meant the same thing? Think about it: *his-story*. Then someone came along and thought it might be good to separate the two and distinguish fact from fiction. Probably a good thing, but just goes to show how closely related those two things really are."

Viviani sighed. *She* knew the two were related. The magic they shared was quite apparent to her, thank you very much.

"Not the answer you were looking for, eh, Firecracker?" Papa said. "Let me give it some more thought."

Viviani and her papa painted walls and fixed the pulley on a dumbwaiter and fished a clump of gum from the water fountain. The lion hanging over it was practically frowning until the drain was cleared; then, Viviani imagined, when it was fixed, he went back to sleep, purring. Viv and her papa wound the clocks, and they cleaned and polished the pneumatic tubes. Last, they unclogged toilets.

"This is worse than prison," Viviani said, her lip curled while plunging the pot.

"Ah, but no! Let me tell you a little story about prison. It all goes back to when I was a boxer. A real palooka, I was . . . ," Papa replied, and he shadowboxed, throwing punches and uppercuts into thin air, wearing his rubbery work gloves and flinging toilet water about. Viviani laughed and forgot all about the smell and the stink and the ick. Papa's stories could do that.

After a day of fix-its and storytelling, Viviani was feeling less like a fizzle and more like a flame again.

"Last chore, Firecracker," Papa said, squeezing her in a sideways hug. "Gotta stoke the furnace."

Viviani's stomach lurched. "The furnace?"

"Yes, ma'am."

"The one in the basement?"

"That's the one."

"I'm not allowed in there."

"You are when you're with me."

The two wound down, down the cold, hard staircase while Viviani's heartbeat sped up, up. The hairs on the back of her neck prickled, and her skin grew cold and goose bumpy. "Papa, I—"

"Come on in," he said, flinging open the door. The air was gritty, strung with shadows. The furnace hissed like a black cat, and Viviani jumped.

Papa unclicked the latch, and the door creaked open. Dry heat blasted their faces, dried out their eyes. Viviani knotted her fingers.

"The shovel, Viv?"

She shook her head. The coal shovel was in the dark corner, unseen.

Papa sighed. "Viviani. Please get the shovel."

Viviani stayed glued to the spot. The heavy door clanged shut behind her.

Her father knelt. "Viviani," he said. "Are you feeling scared right now?"

Viviani nodded. Her heart raced.

"I heard Merit talking to you in your room last night. Think about how scared you are right now—that's how you purposely tried to make your friend Merit feel. You can tell stories all you want, my love. But you can't do it with malice. You asked earlier what makes the difference between a liar and a storyteller?"

Viviani nodded slowly, tears stinging her eyes.

"I believe it's intent. What you *intend* to do with your stories. If your plan all along was to scare Merit, well . . ."

He sighed. "You're not a liar, Viviani. But you did do something dishonest."

Viviani couldn't swallow past the lump in her throat.

"I owe Merit a huge apology," Viviani said, sniffling.

Papa folded Viviani into a warm, strong hug.

The door of the furnace room pounded open. Viviani jolted and whirled toward the entrance.

There stood Mr. Green.

"John!" he said, panting. He'd obviously been running. "Come quick! The stamps—they're missing!"

CHAPTER TWENTY-FIVE

Crime Scenes,

Dewey Decimal 363.25

SEE ALSO: *thievery, criminal investigation*

I hope you've never had the extreme misfortune to witness a tornado, Friend. They are swirling, dirty, dangerous things, and they pick up even the heaviest objects—cows! cars!—and toss them about willy-nilly. And once they've passed, they leave a trail of garbage and debris in their wake.

That is what the third-floor display room looked like at the moment.

The clear cases were shattered, shards of glass sprinkling the floor like dangerous diamonds. The cleaning crew, led by Mr. Green and a couple of librarians, were blocking off the area until the police arrived. The panic in the room pulsed like a huge, throbbing heartbeat.

"Those stamps were priceless! Priceless!" Miss O'Conner muttered, her glasses barely clinging to the tip of her nose.

"Oh, poor Mr. Smyth is going to be so upset!" another librarian said.

Viviani missed the Inverted Jenny already. It was like a friend moving away. Without saying goodbye.

"See the tape?" Mr. Leon, the daytime guard, said, pointing to the case. The glass had remnants of sticky goo smudged on it in several spots. "That clear stuff—it's new. You don't see that stuff everywhere. The thief knew to use it to keep the sound muffled, so no one would hear the glass breaking. And the timing. It was almost as if the thief knew Mr. Eames's routine down to his every footfall. The person who did this? They knew exactly what they were doing and how to sneak around the library."

Mr. Green's gaze shifted onto Viviani. He'd caught her doing exactly that just hours ago. She gulped.

Miss O'Conner stood nearby, toe tapping. "Missing, just like those picture books. Someone is having a time in this library, indeed."

Viviani couldn't help but think the comment was directed at her.

Mr. Leon coughed. "A couple of missing picture books hardly compares to these stamps, Miss O'Conner."

Her eyes went wide behind her spectacles. "Is that so? Perhaps monetarily they differ. But picture books build readers, Mr. Leon. Two missing books from our collection is like two missing bricks from a cathedral." She crammed those glasses up the bridge of her nose so hard, Viviani thought surely she'd embedded them in her flesh permanently.

Mr. Eames, Viviani's night guard friend, the keeper of the Master Thief tally, paced the room, knotting and unknotting his fingers. "I didn't hear a thing," he muttered. "I didn't see anything, I didn't hear anything. . . ."

Viviani crossed over to him. "Mr. Eames?" He stopped pacing and smiled weakly at her. Today's bow tie was a cheery red plaid. "Are you okay?"

"I think . . . I think I'm going to lose my job, Viviani."

Viviani's heart twisted. Mr. Eames had a wife, two kids, and three grandkids at home. He needed every penny of his salary!

Mr. Leon circled the wreckage, looking at the ceiling, the doors, shining a weak flashlight beam everywhere, even though sunshine streamed through the windows. "Yes, the burglar knew exactly where to go. Whoever knows how to wander the building like this at night is most certainly the thief."

Viviani's head swirled like the tornado of chaos she saw in front of her.

And by the way Mr. Green glared at her, she knew he thought she was responsible.

Dear Friend,

The stamps are missing—gone!—and my terrible day just got terribler and terribler. After talking to Mr. Green, Dr. Anderson marched up to Papa and said, "Would your children know anything about this, Fedeler?"

There were some mumblings, some head nods—the kinds of things adults do when they don't want kids to hear. But I did catch Dr. Anderson telling Papa, "If you find out your children are involved in any way, Fedeler, you'll lose your job, you know."

Papa straightened and nodded. "I know."

Friend, if a person could fly just by blinking, I'd be in China after that; I blinked back that many tears overhearing those words.

Our dinner tonight was question after question after question, and John Jr., Edouard, and I told them everything we knew. We even brought them to the spot where we heard the moaning the night before (yes, I trembled like a malt machine, but I did it). We found nothing.

Nothing.

Mr. Eames might lose his job.

Papa might lose his job.

Papa losing his job is worse than him being out of work.

Papa losing his job means that we'll lose our home.

I'll lose the library.

I have to find out what happened.

I'm going to find out who—or WHAT—took those stamps.

I just hope Big Red stays out of our way.

CHAPTER TWENTY-SIX

Suspects,

Dewey Decimal 364.15

SEE ALSO: *accused, guilty, criminal behavior*

A LIST OF SUSPECTS by Viviani Joffre Fedeler

1. ~~MR. EAMES.~~ ←He does have access, but nah—far too nice. Although he does seem to know a lot about Master Thief . . .
2. **MR. LEON?** Mr. Eames once told me the night shift makes more money than the day shift. Could he be after Mr. Eames's job?
3. **THE DOUGHNUT SISTERS!** Hoo boy, those ladies hate those stamps!
4. **MR. SMYTH?** Papa told a story once where the owner "stole" his own stuff to get "insurance money." (Note to self: ask what this is.)

5. **DR. ANDERSON.** He sure seemed to know exactly how much money those stamps were worth and seemed awfully impressed by it.

6. **ANY.** Mr. Wilburforce, maybe. Or that Miss O'Conner. No one ever suspects a librarian.

7. **~~JAKE JOSEPH~~.** ←Only kidding, of course. Still mad at him for that whole snowball thing.

8. **CARROLL CASE?** It's ridiculous, but he's the only one of us who is *not* family and who wasn't with me the whole time. Because it couldn't be . . .

9. **~~EVA OR MERIT?~~** ←Eva, impossible. IMPOSSIBLE. Even less likely than Mr. Eames. But Merit . . . maybe she wanted to get back at me? She went to the restroom once, but was it long enough to steal the stamps? Highly doubtful.

10. **BIG RED**?!?!?!

11. **MR. GREEN.** *** MOST LIKELY SUSPECT #1!!! HIM telling on US is a great cover-up. Plus no one ever hears him, and he's up to something with that locked closet of his. Just watch, Friend. It's time to catch a thief.

CHAPTER TWENTY-SEVEN

Negotiation,

Dewey Decimal 303.69

SEE ALSO: *conflict management, conflict resolutions*

A s the daughter of the library superintendent, Viviani had seen things get fixed her whole life: a burned-out bulb? Screw in a new one. A fizzled fuse? Replace it. A loose bolt? Tighten it.

Fix. Repair. Strengthen.

And so, Viviani Joffre Fedeler knew that this situation—the missing stamps, the furious friends— needed fixing. But she couldn't do it alone. She needed help. And the more she thought about it, she knew she needed the help of someone as brave and as fearless as herself.

She needed Merit.

Eva told Viviani that Merit's apartment was a block and a half past the school and several blocks down First Avenue. The low gray sky was spitting snow, and the ice pellets stung Viviani's cheeks as she walked the cold, wide sidewalks. She huddled into the prickly fox fur collar on her coat. As Viviani got closer to Merit's building, her skin felt electrified with the constant hum of the Edison power plants lined up like soldiers along the East River. Black coal smoke churned into the air, and she soon felt covered in grit.

Merit's apartment was located between a house sporting a sign that read RUSSIAN & TURKISH BATHS & HEALTH CLUB SINCE 1892 (Viv could hear Mama gasp from here) and a set of musky-smelling horse stables. As she wound her way up the creaky wooden stairs to the sixth floor, she smelled meat frying, heard the sizzle and clank of fire and pans. Her stomach grumbled. She knocked.

A little girl who looked a lot like Merit swung open the door. She blinked up at Viviani. Viv gave her warmest smile.

"Is your big sister here?"

The girl shrugged.

"Eshe! Who is it?"

Merit's mother rounded the corner, wiping her hands on an apron. Viviani had never seen a lovelier woman: stunning and strong, with thick black hair piled atop her head. Mrs. Mubarak wore a colorful dress that reminded Viviani of the illustrations found in books about botanical flowers. She smiled at Viviani. "Can I help you?"

"I'm here to see Merit, ma'am. I'm—" Viviani paused and, for the first time ever, thought introducing herself by name might not be a good idea. "I'm a schoolmate of Merit's."

"A schoolmate. I see. Have a seat. I'll get Merit. Would you like some *kofta*?"

"If that's what smells so amazing, then absolutely."

Mrs. Mubarak laughed, which made Viviani feel like she was passing through a ray of sunshine. "It is. I'll get you some."

She swept back to the kitchen. Viviani perched on the edge of the couch and glanced around the room: a fire danced in the fireplace, a kitten purred on a cushion nearby. It was warm, and light, and every inch was covered with pillows and blankets. The library was magical and luxurious and all, but . . . here was all fluff and cotton and *cush*.

Until Merit entered.

Merit's eyes dashed around the room, as though she were embarrassed by it. Then she crossed her arms.

"What do you want, *Red*?" Her voice stung like the ice pellets falling from the gray skies outside. Viviani knew Merit was making a dig at how Viv had turned out to be the ghost. At least, that's what Merit thought.

Viviani sighed. "You. I want your help. And please don't call me Red anymore."

"I think you can find someone else to help. Your brothers seem all too willing."

Viviani shook her head. "Not on this. They don't love those stamps like we do."

"The stamps? What happened?"

As Viviani explained about the missing stamp collection, Merit slowly, carefully sat opposite her, eyes widening.

"They're—*gone*?" Merit asked. "The Inverted Jenny, too?"

"Yep. All of them. Stolen."

At that moment, Mrs. Mubarak returned with a plate of steaming *kofta*. Viviani lifted a skewer and took a bite of the meat. "Wow! What are these called again? Heaven on a stick?"

Merit's lips pulled to the side of her face to hold back her laughter because she didn't wish to give Viviani the satisfaction of chuckling at her joke. Mrs. Mubarak laughed, though. "*Kofta*. Here, let me get you some *basbousa*, too."

Viviani looked over her shoulder, making sure Mrs. Mubarak was well behind the swinging kitchen door, out of earshot. "I need your help, Merit," Viviani whispered. "I want to figure out who did this. I need to do this for"—her voice faltered—"for my papa."

Merit chewed her bottom lip, played with her left earring. Viviani had envied those pierced ears since the first time she saw them. Viviani Joffre Fedeler wasn't used to the uncomfortable itchiness of envy.

"Merit," she said, inhaling deeply. Then the words tumbled out like pages fanning by in a thumbed paperback: "I'm sorry. I'm sorry I tried to trick you. It was wrong. I thought it'd be fun. I thought I'd show you how much fun it can be to believe in something with your heart, even though you don't believe it with your head. I wanted to show you the difference between a lie and a story. And, well . . . it ended up still being a lie."

Merit's eyes softened. Mrs. Mubarak showed up just then and placed a huge piece of yellow cake in front of Viv. It smelled sweet, like roses, and it tasted like honey and spun sunshine.

"Mrs. Mubarak!" Viviani said around a mouthful of food, forgetting her manners entirely. "This is amazing!

Can you please give my mama this recipe? She's a great cook—I know she'd love this!"

"I'd be happy to!" Mrs. Mubarak smiled and scooped up Merit's little sister, who Viviani had forgotten was nearby. Eshe was so quiet. Not like Viv's siblings at all!

Merit finished her piece of cake and stood. "Mama, I'm going to walk Viviani home. We have things to talk about."

The two girls bundled and double-bundled and walked through the sleet back to the library. Outside the massive building, Merit paused and placed her hand on one of the lions, now gathering ice in its mane.

"That's Leo Lenox," Viviani said. "Named after one of the guys who started the library. Papa won't let us have a dog or a cat in the building, so I kinda think of him as my pet."

Merit nodded and stroked the stone lion. Maybe Viviani's imagination was winning her over?

Viviani stroked his mane, too. "I like to think he's out here with his brother, Leo Astor over there, making sure all of New York is protected and safe."

"He didn't do a very good job last night."

"No. Lions sleep, too, sometimes."

"A catnap, then," Merit said, and Viviani burst out laughing. Her heart filled with hope that Merit was coming around.

Merit sighed and looked up at the six huge columns on the front of the library, lined up like books on shelves. "Listen, Viviani: I'm still not sure if we can be friends. You lied to me and tricked me. But I'll do it. I'll help you find that thief."

Viviani couldn't stop herself: she threw her bundled arms around Merit and pressed her cold cheek against Merit's warm one. "What made you change your mind? Was it my sincerity? My positivity? My imagination? My sense of humor?"

Merit fought a smile. "It was none of the above. I simply can't resist a good mystery."

"I'll take it. For now." Viviani smiled, then sobered. "But I hope we can be friends someday."

"Maybe someday," Merit said softly. Then she scratched her chin. "Do you know of a place where we can get photographs developed?"

Viviani bounced on her toes. "Know of a place? I live in that place."

CHAPTER TWENTY-EIGHT

Photography,

Dewey Decimal 770.28

SEE ALSO: *photography equipment and supplies*

The door to the Printing Office creaked open, and three girls peeked inside: Viviani, Merit, and Eva, who'd joined the group after they made a short detour to Rogers Peet to recruit her. The air was dark and cool, and no one stood behind the large oak counter. The Printing Office was in the basement, and being down here, so close to where they had heard the moaning, so close to where the furnace banged and the pistons popped and Mr. Green kept his mysterious closet locked tight—well, the three girls were as jittery as gelatin.

Viviani *dinged* the brass bell on the counter, and

still—no one. She *dingdingdingdinge*d it, and at last, a door in the back corner swung open.

"I'm coming, I'm coming," a voice echoed, and then the speaker appeared. It was Mr. Tuttle, and Viviani thought he was perhaps the most appropriately named fellow she'd ever met: his back was hunched, he moved at a glacial pace, and he always, always wore a bright green visor.

"Viviani!" he bellowed, his face lighting up. "To what do I owe this honor, neighbor?"

"Mr. Tuttle," Viviani whispered, and looked over her shoulder. If her father heard her asking for this favor, his disapproving grumble might shake the whole island of Manhattan. "My friends"—here Merit shifted uneasily—"and I need to get some film developed. Quickly. Can you help us?"

Mr. Tuttle lowered the brim of his visor, as if he were conspiring with them. "I'm only supposed to develop photographs for the library, Miss Fedeler."

"Oh, this will help the library!" Viviani said. "We think."

"We think, eh?" Mr. Tuttle tugged at the loose skin of his neck. "Well, that's good enough for me. Let's go."

Eva, Merit, and Viviani each gave Mr. Tuttle a quick hug, then followed him down the hall.

"Film is developed in complete darkness, you see," Mr. Tuttle said, shuffling slowly toward a door marked DARKROOM. "It's very dark overall. You cannot open the door at first, or the film will be ruined. If you'd prefer to wait out here, you can. Understand?"

The girls exchanged excited glances. "We'd all like to go, please," Merit piped up. Her voice had music and smiles and bounce woven within it, and Viviani could tell she was filled to the brim with joy about watching film get developed.

The darkroom was small and cold and smelled like powerful chemicals—bitter and biting, like the scent of vinegar. One long table lined with shallow silver trays and brown bottles was the only furniture in the room.

"Last warning," Mr. Tuttle said. "If you don't like darkness, I'd recommend waiting outside."

Viviani half expected Eva to spin on her heel and march out, but she stayed. Mr. Tuttle banged the metal door shut, and Viviani gasped.

This wasn't the kind of darkness Viviani had experienced to this point in her eleven years. This wasn't just darkness; this was a complete and utter lack of light. Smothering. Heavy, as if it actually *weighed* something. And there were no shadows. None. Darkness this thick swallowed everything whole.

Breathe, Viviani, she told herself. But the chemical air stung her lungs. *Breathe*.

"First, we open the back of the camera," Mr. Tuttle was saying. There were clicks and whirs, but Viviani couldn't see a thing. "I'm using the winding key to roll the film onto a spool pin," Mr. Tuttle explained.

"A spool pin," Merit whispered, as if committing this experience to memory.

Viviani's head spun. Mr. Tuttle said some things about solutions and developer and temperatures, and he seemed very happy to have an audience in this small dark room.

Small. Dark. Room. Viviani's throat tightened.

". . . and then we'll use a solution called stop bath," Mr. Tuttle was saying as he banged and clanged in the darkness.

"Stop bath," Eva said with a laugh, from somewhere to Viv's left. "Sounds like something John Jr. would use, right, Viv?"

Viviani attempted a half-hearted chuckle.

"Are you okay, Viviani?" Merit asked.

It was so odd, these voices from the dark!

"I'm okay!" she said, likely too loud, but her ears were ringing, so it was difficult to tell if she was shouting.

"Would you like to sit on the floor, Miss Fedeler?" Mr. Tuttle asked. "If you need to leave . . ."

"No, I'm okay," Viviani shouted. "We cannot ruin that film." She sank to the floor. From there, she listened to them discussing fix bath and more agitating and rinsing and drying agents.

Viviani heard Mr. Tuttle drop the film into a hollow canister, then pour in some bitter-smelling chemicals. She heard him screw a cap on, and then he flipped on a small, red-toned light. After all that darkness, the pale light felt blinding. Mr. Tuttle turned the canister upside down, then upright again. "Are you okay, Miss Fedeler? You can leave now if you—"

"I'm okay!" Viviani said in a bit of a whimper from the floor. "I'm fine!"

Mr. Tuttle nodded. "Merit? Would you like to agitate the film for us?"

"Would I! My sister would probably tell you I'm very good at agitating things."

Eva and Mr. Tuttle laughed. Merit flipped the canister up and down, up and down, between her hands, the solution inside sloshing. Sloshing like Viviani's insides. Ugh. Her stomach felt bitter.

For the longest eight and a half minutes of Viviani's life, Merit and Eva took turns sloshing the canister around. They seemed startled when Viviani passed on taking a turn.

"Okay, girls. Now, we dump out the developing solution"—Viviani had closed her eyes at this point, so she didn't see where the solution went—"and we douse the film in . . ."

The room felt as if it were closing in on Viviani, just like in Poe's "Cask of Amontillado." The story was about a man tricked into a deep, dark cellar and then . . . stone by stone—oh! Why would she think of that *now*? Cursed imagination.

Something clanged in the depth of this small darkroom.

"A hammer!" Viviani whimpered, and photographs ready or not, she pushed through the door of the darkroom and into the blinding bright lights of the Printing Office.

CHAPTER TWENTY-NINE

Crime,

Dewey Decimal 364

SEE ALSO: *crime and criminals, crime and detection*

Viviani groaned when Merit and Eva found her sulking in her bedroom some time later.

"I ruined the photographs," she said to the floor, her head between her knees. "I am so sorry I ruined the photographs."

Merit and Eva shared a grin. "No, you didn't, Viviani. They're down there drying now. Come on!"

Viviani leapt up, her dizziness forgotten.

"Thank goodness! Well, let's look at them!"

The trio dashed down one, two flights of stairs and into the Printing Office. Hanging in the back on a clothesline, their smiling mugs: Eva tossing her head back in laughter while scaling a bookshelf. Merit looking deadly serious as she talked to the president on a telephone. Viviani riding atop a book cart, finger held aloft, conqueror of the library.

Mr. Tuttle *ahemed*. "I'll pretend I saw none of this, girls."

Viviani hugged Mr. Tuttle. He tugged at the skin on his neck and said, "Your friends tell me you're looking for clues in these photos, Miss Fedeler. Perhaps these tools might help." He opened his hand, and there he held a magnifying glass and two loops—the magnifying eyepieces scholars and jewelers wear to study things closely.

Merit squealed.

Merit *squealing*? Viviani smiled. There was a shot at friendship yet. "Thank you, Mr. Tuttle! I'll return them to you in perfect condition."

Mr. Tuttle smiled. "Don't mention it. Those tools are available to anyone who visits the library. Surely that goes doubly for you, neighbor."

The girls raced upstairs and found a quiet nook near a massive card catalog on the second floor. They began flipping through the photographs.

"Look at this one of Eva spinning in the office chairs!" Viviani giggled and pointed to Eva's wild grin, her flying hair. "You look like a bearcat!"

Eva laughed. "But you in this photo, Viv! Sliding down the banister like that. Now I finally have proof to show your mother."

The photos showed Viviani silhouetted against a tall window browsing the large display dictionary. Eva turning cartwheels in the wide second-floor hallway. Merit posing like a famous singer at the WJZ microphone. The girls laughed as they relived the sleepover through Merit's photos.

"That was a pretty fun night." Merit sighed while looking at a photo of herself sitting on a throne of books. Viviani smiled. It *had* been a fun night.

Finally, Viviani took a deep breath, and they flipped to the photo of John Jr. just as he'd leapt out from behind the bookstacks, dressed as Big Red. At the time, Merit's flash had blinded them all, taken in the darkness. The photo she'd captured of John Jr. showed him wild-eyed, hair mussed. The fake beard was crooked, glued on so that it looked more like an orange tabby cat stuck to his pale, freckled jaw. The coveralls Viv had "borrowed" from Papa for the stunt sagged at his wrists, his ankles, and his mouth puckered, as if saying *Red*.

No one said a word. Viviani felt her cheeks burn in shame. Oh, Merit must really hate her.

Merit was the first to giggle. "He certainly looks as if he's seen a ghost," she chuckled.

Eva began to laugh, too. "And look! There's Carroll, peeking out of the stacks behind him!"

Viviani leaned in over the girls, and she hovered the magnifying glass over the photograph. Sure enough, Carroll's thick curly hair and two flashing white eyes poked out from behind a bookshelf. The girls screamed with laughter, and a faraway librarian shushed them.

They laughed until tears streamed down their faces. They laughed until their stomachs hurt. They laughed until they were giggling piles of mush.

As they were catching their breath, Merit gasped. "Look! Right there!"

The trio focused their attention where Merit had pointed. In the upper right corner of the photo, barely peeking out from behind a bookshelf: the heel of a shoe.

A running-away shoe.

But twisted at an odd angle, like it was being dragged.

"Ghosts don't wear shoes," Eva whispered.

Merit shook her head. "Nope. But thieves do."

"I know that shoe." Viviani scratched her chin, then dug back through the pile of photographs until she reached the one that Merit had taken of the Inverted Jenny.

And, yep. She saw the same shoe.

CHAPTER THIRTY

Traps,

Dewey Decimal 639.1

SEE ALSO: *snares, ambushes*

Dear Friend,

A new day, a new plan.

I feel excited and nervous and eager and jittery all at once like some of the herky-jerky, sparky inventions that Papa fiddles with in his workshop. We're going to catch a thief.

The thief is still here—I know it. The odd angle of that shoe, the moan we heard: that thief is still here, and struggling.

I keep telling Eva—and myself—it's sorta

like capturing fireflies. Unpredictable but not dangerous.

I hope I'm right.

We decided not to tell Mama and Papa about this plan because, well, they're already concerned for his job, for our home. And this one? It's all on me, Friend, I'm sorry to say. When I saw that shoe, I realized: I did this.

I got us into this, and I'm going to get us out.

Merit and Eva arrived at the library for sleepover number two. Because it was winter break, multiple sleepovers a week were possible, and those were the best kinds of weeks of all. Viviani had to agree to months of extra chores to garner another sleepover so soon after the last one had ended in a jumbled pile of hijinks, but Mama, ever the hostess, caved eventually.

Eva lugged in her heavy, bulging-at-the-zipper suitcase, dragging it across the floor behind her. When Mama raised an eyebrow at it, Merit shrugged and said, "Viviani had an idea for a craft."

"Carry on," Mama said, for she was quite used to Viviani's ideas for things.

And once again, the shadows crept across the great, wide expanse of floor. And the ticks of the clock in the Main Reading Room swept by like passing librarians.

At midnight, Viviani pressed her ear to the door of her parents' room. Papa was snoring like a dragon, and Mama's nose was whistling. The sound-asleep symphony.

"Let's go," Viviani said, motioning her head to the door.

It creaked open. Viviani wished John Jr. or Carroll or Edouard had agreed to help, but they were still too mad at her for getting them in trouble after last time. Viviani had never before had so many people mad at her at once. It felt awful, like the stomach flu, only worse because you couldn't just gulp down some cod liver oil and get it all out already.

Tonight, no one slid down banisters. The three girls padded down the stairs, Eva lugging her heavy bag behind her *clunk clunk clunk*. Was it Viviani's imagination, or was the library getting colder the farther they went into the dark?

Viviani wished she knew the routine of Mr. Leon. He had taken over the night shift, at least until it could be proved that Mr. Eames was indeed doing his job the evening the stamps went missing. But, no: Viv would just have to hope that their paths did not cross.

Soon they were again near the drippy, windowless basement, again approaching the clanging that sounded an awful lot like a hammer, again with heartbeats louder than footsteps. Viviani clicked on the Ray-O-Vac flashlight. It puttered on, a pale yellow beam leading the way.

"*Unnnggghhh!*" came a sound through the darkness.

"Shhh!" Merit said, freezing, readying her camera. "Did you hear that?"

Viviani gulped, nodded.

Merit glared at Viviani, her eyes shining in the flashlight beam. "Viv, this is your last chance. You need to let me know right now if this is another prank. . . ."

Viviani shook her head and drew an *X* across her chest. "Cross my heart and hope to die."

Eva whimpered. "Please no dying tonight, okay?"

The girls padded down three more cold, hard steps. "*Ooof!*"

The thing—*the thief*, Viv thought—had run into something. That couldn't be a ghost, then, could it? No, of course not. Viviani knew this wasn't a ghost now. The girls exchanged glances. No one wanted to be the one to call off the mission, so they continued.

Down, down, down.

"Eva, get ready," Viviani whispered. Eva zipped open her bag. The zipper sounded like fabric ripping in all this darkness, like sharp claws tearing through a shirt. Eva fished out her handiwork.

The trio tiptoed through the maze of bookstacks, weaving around the bases of the seven-level shelves that spanned the entire back side of the building. Bookstacks loomed over them like silent giants.

The girls turned the corner around a tall shelf and—

There!

A dark figure, stumbling. Limping.

Just like in Papa's story! Just like Big Red himself!

But Viviani knew this wasn't a ghost. This was a thief. A thief she knew.

Viviani gulped and shouted:

"NOW!"

CHAPTER THIRTY-ONE

Surprises,

Dewey Decimal 152.4

SEE ALSO: *unpredictable, unexpected*

A word about *nows*:

Some *nows* truly do feel as sudden and sharp as the word itself: "NOW!" Like when you're trying to swat a fly, or capture lightning on film. But some *nows*, somehow, draw out the *O* so that a breathy instant feels more like an eternity: "NOOOOOOOOOOOOOOOOOOOW!"

The girls felt the latter, as if they were slowly moving through water.

They hurled Eva's horribly crocheted blanket over the dark, lumbering figure. Merit took one end of the skein of yarn and circled the form, tightening the net around it. Tighter, tighter. The thing groaned.

Viviani leapt forward, crochet needle in hand. "AHA!" she shouted. As she did so, she nudged a nearby shelf of books, and the books toppled onto the figure, *thud, thump, CRASH!* The thing moaned even louder and stumbled forward.

Eva screamed.

"Confess!" Viviani shouted at the trapped figure. "Give us those stamps you stole!"

Viviani swirled the flashlight up toward the figure, just as the overhead light clicked on.

"What in the world is going on in here?"

Mr. Green stood in the doorway, his approach silent as always. The cannibal himself, looming over them. Viviani didn't know she could be more scared than she'd just been, but sure enough, her stomach churned and her palms grew sweaty.

"You girls wandering around this library will be the death of me, you hear? And what with that recent thievery, too. You have me worried sick."

Worried sick?

Mr. Green looked at the trio of girls holding a skein of yarn, a crochet needle, and the hem of a horrible blanket. He then saw someone struggling beneath the loose pile of yarn. He leapt forward and yanked the blanket off. The thief's leg was bent at a grotesque angle.

He clutched a large envelope and wore a terrible pea-soup coat.

Mr. Hill.

Viviani had hoped she wasn't right—that the shoes in the photo next to the Inverted Jenny and the shoes in the photo of John Jr. dressed as Big Red were just a coincidence. But, no, photos don't lie. Merit loved that about photography. Photos tells facts. Tears welled in Viv's eyes as Mr. Hill avoided her gaze.

Sometimes the bad guy is disguised as a good guy.

Does that mean . . . that sometimes the good guy looks like a bad guy?

Mr. Green snatched the envelope from Mr. Hill and shook it open. Sure enough, the missing stamps were inside.

"Well, I'll be," Mr. Green snarled. "It seems you girls have caught yourselves a burglar."

CHAPTER THIRTY-TWO

Justice,

Dewey Decimal 172.2

SEE ALSO: *common good, fairness*

Justice! They'd caught the thief. The feeling of doing something right made Viviani feel extra jolty, just like jazzy radio songs or the first sunny spring day. The feeling was too much to contain: Viviani, Merit, and Eva ran to the tip-top of the library, then slid and skidded down every banister in sight, whooping and hollering and waking the entire family, thank you very much.

It was, of course, bittersweet for Viv. Yes, she'd saved Mr. Eames's job. Yes, she'd saved Papa's job and their home in the library. But Mr. Hill had tricked her, just as she'd tried tricking Merit, and, boy, did it feel terrible. And as she soon discovered, his name wasn't even Mr. Hill at all.

"Joseph Hemphill," he said, extending his hand to Viviani again, this time in apology. The whole Fedeler clan was downstairs awaiting the police. She thought about not shaking his hand; she truly did. But this fellow had helped her realize that her story was worth telling. That her voice was worth listening to. That she was, indeed, a story collector. And so she shook it. And as she did, she said, "You know what, Mr. Hill? I mean, Mr. Hemphill? You're not a bad-luck collector. It seems to me you create your own bad luck."

The police came and cuffed Mr. Joseph Hemphill, dragging him off cursing and limping. The night he'd stolen the stamps, he'd heard the kids wandering the library and thought it was the guards. He'd made his way to the basement and tried to scale the card catalog in the library school ("the best hiding spot," Viviani had told him) but had tumbled backward and broken his leg. He'd been unable to escape the library after that, hiding and wandering the stacks, dragging his leg through the basement.

"So, see, Papa?" Viviani said to him. "Our wandering the library at night actually *saved* the stamps."

Based on Papa's frown, he wasn't buying that line of logic.

As it turns out, the crash that the kids had heard that night when John Jr. was dressed as Big Red? A too tightly stretched electrical cord, spanning from a telegraph machine wrapped in tinfoil to the far wall. Viviani and Eva's Martian communicator in Papa's workshop. Mr. Hill—Mr. *Hemphill*—had tripped over it. They'd set a trap without even knowing it.

"So, see, Papa?" Viviani said again. "My playing in the workshop was pretty handy after all."

Based on Papa's deepening frown, Viviani decided to stop pointing out all the ways she'd helped.

Viviani, Merit, and Eva had their picture taken for the newspaper. *Pop!* went the photographer's loud flash, which blinded them and left them blinking back red stars for many minutes.

"It'll be in tomorrow's paper," the reporter grunted as he left. Viviani wondered if Mr. Hemphill had even been a reporter at all that first day, on the steps of the library. She doubted it. Had he paid for her fancy leather captain's log, or had he stolen that, too? Oh, she had so many questions for him, but she figured most of those would remain unanswered.

Perhaps she'd just have to make up stories to fill in the blanks.

"Oh, Viv," Mama said, sighing, after most of the excitement had died down. She pulled Viviani in for a tight hug and breathed in her scent, as mamas do. "I'm so glad you girls are safe."

John Jr. ruffled her hair, and Edouard said, "Fact: that was stupid but I'm glad you're okay." Then he punched her on the arm.

Papa hugged her hardest of all, a hug that felt like all the safety and light and warmth in the world. "Nice work, kid."

"Yeah?"

"Yes. And you're in big trouble. We're talking weeks of extra chores, Firecracker."

Viviani smiled. Weeks of spending more time with Papa sounded like just the punishment she needed. "You can start calling me Red again, you know."

Papa grabbed her chin and jostled it. "Yeah?"

John Jr. shook his head. "Naw, Firecracker is the bee's knees. Let's keep that."

"But what if I don't want to be called that?"

John Jr. trapped her in a gentle headlock and tickled her. "Like you have a choice in your own nickname, Firecracker."

The next night, the bow tie–sporting Mr. Eames wandered and whistled through the hallways once again, but now, much to John Jr.'s and Edouard's and Viviani's dismay, he changed up his routine. They knew that from this point forward, they'd never know where he'd be, and when. Their Master Thief tallies would be doomed, and their snooping and sneaking would be that much more difficult. (Note that it by no means *squelched* the snooping and sneaking.)

And speaking of sneaking: Viviani just *had* to know. So later that same day, after all the hubbub, she gathered her gumption and faced her fears head-on. She found the custodian in the map room and tapped him on the shoulder.

"Mr. Green?"

The cleaning man spun around, his messy blond hair falling over one glaring green eye. "Yeah?"

Viviani swallowed. "Um, I was wondering. How come everyone's shoes make so much noise in this library but yours? How come we never hear you coming?"

Mr. Green scowled down at his glossy wing tips. "The shine, don'cha know? Makes 'em soft. These here shoes are like ballet slippers, they are."

The idea of the janitor wearing ballet slippers made Viviani laugh. Mr. Green did not. He turned to empty another special lion-emblazoned library garbage can. But that wasn't the question she truly wished to ask.

"Mr. Green?"

He grunted, which Viviani took as permission to keep speaking.

Viviani took the INVENTORS' CLUB sign from her pocket. "Did you get me in trouble with my parents because of this sign?"

Mr. Green paused and looked at the note Viviani was smoothing flat over the glossy table in the map room.

"I'm sorry I . . . called you a cannibal," Viviani whispered.

"You did what?" Mr. Green's face shifted. It was the first time Viv had seen him do anything other than scowl. She imagined his face muscles creaking and groaning and moaning before landing in a somewhat awkward grin.

"Right here," Viviani said, and tapped the note. "The cannibal part. I'm sorry I—"

But Viviani halted midsentence, which was a rare thing indeed, for her to run out of words like that. Then she saw it: the way Mr. Green looked at the note, like it was a thing made of magic instead of ink and paper.

"Mr. Green," Viviani asked slowly, "can you read?"

Mr. Green's face looked wistful, as if he were seeing something far away, rather than the window in the map room. He didn't answer, which was, of course, his answer.

His face twitched. "Follow me."

Mr. Green slid through the library as silently as a ghost, Viviani trailing behind him. He wound down, down, down to the basement and stopped just in front of his rusted, locked-tight custodial closet. He dug for his key.

The key. His one-of-a-kind, special, nobody-else-has-one key.

Viviani's insides shriveled. Her heart raced. This was a mistake, starting this conversation. Asking if he could read. He had led her to *the* closet. He was searching for *the* key.

He found the key and swiftly unlocked the door, which likely held back an entire arsenal of weaponry. Or organs floating in yellowy jars. Or entrails. He swung the door open. It shrieked on its hinges. Something toppled off a shelf and landed on Viviani's toe. She yelped and leapt backward. Was it a saw? A bone? A skull?

It was a picture book.

"You're the culprit?" Viviani said, picking up the book from the ground. "You've been stealing picture books from the children's room!"

"Not stealing," Mr. Green grumbled. "Borrowing. I always return 'em." He snatched the book, called *Millions of Cats*, from Viviani. It was new, and he was dusting it off, inspecting it to make certain it hadn't been damaged in the fall.

"The pictures, see. I'm teaching myself using the books with the pictures. This one's about cats." He pointed to the word *cats*.

"You could check them out with a library card, Mr. Green," Viviani said, but Mr. Green was already shaking his head.

"Can't fill out the form."

Viviani's heart twisted. Oh, to be unable to swim inside written stories! To not have them woven about your heart! To spend so much of your life in a library and not be able to enjoy its offerings! Viviani felt that the absence of books in Mr. Green's life must be like color blindness, or like constantly wearing itchy wet wool in summer, or like the inability to taste sugar or salt.

"I'm going to teach you to read, Mr. Green," Viviani said, chin lifted. "We'll begin our lessons tomorrow. In the map room. Bring a pen and a piece of paper."

Mr. Green's face lit up, but he shuffled his feet. "Now, the miss don't need to go and do that."

Viviani smiled and considered all the stories Mr. Green would be able to unlock with *this* key. This special, one-of-a-kind key: the unique mix of books and stories that *he* would choose to read. Different from everyone else on the planet. *His* blanks to fill in. *His* Once Upon a Time.

"Yes, Mr. Green, I do."

CHAPTER THIRTY-THREE

Friendship,

Dewey Decimal 158.25

SEE ALSO: *best friends, friendship anecdotes*

The following day, the *New York Daily News* featured a photo of Viviani, Merit, and Eva with the headline LIBRARY MOPPETS STAMP OUT STAMP THIEF. Merit's father was so proud that he ran out and grabbed every copy he could find. He made Merit bring three extra copies to the library for Viviani.

She plunked the stack in front of Viv. "That could've been very dangerous, Viviani."

Viv shrank. Here it came: the part where Merit decided they couldn't be friends anymore, that they were too different to be chums. And then Viv would likely lose all her friends at school, too, once they heard this whopper, once they found out Viviani had dressed up her brother like a ghost. Viviani's eyes stung; she lightly ran her fingers over the photo of their three giddy faces, printed on page one in black and white.

Viviani nodded, agreeing at last. "It was dangerous. I see three lucky girls in this picture."

Merit leaned over her shoulder. "Three lucky girls? I see a Brain," she pointed to herself in the photo, and Viviani laughed. "A Sweetheart." Here, Merit pointed to Eva, and Viviani nodded. "And a Friend."

Viviani perked up. "Yeah? There's a Friend in that photo?"

Merit grinned. "I think so."

Viviani tapped the stack of newspapers. "Photos don't lie, you know. You said it yourself, Brain. If there's a Friend there, that's a fact."

Merit laughed. "The good thing about being the Brain is that I'm always learning. Yes, certainly, photos capture facts." Merit circled the photo with her finger sheepishly. "But they also tell a story. Part of one, at least. I think you should write this story down, Viviani. The story of this photo. *Our* story."

Viviani squealed and threw her arms around Merit. "You got it, Brain."

"Thanks, Friend."

Dear Friend,

Once upon a time there were three girls who caught a thief, a thief who taught one of those girls that her story was worth sharing.

And somehow, everything turned out all right: Papa's and Mr. Eames's jobs were saved, John Jr. and Edouard are no longer mad at me, and best of all, I have another new best friend! Oh, and Mr. Green doesn't want to gobble me up. Maybe. It sure sounds like a Happily Ever After to me.

I am disappointed in one thing, though, if I'm being honest: the fact that there doesn't appear to be a ghost wandering the library stacks at night after all. It had been downright thrilling, thinking of that red-whiskered fellow, gripping his hammer and seeking revenge on the mischief-makers within. Big Red was just a story, I suppose, and while stories often feel real, they may only be true to our hearts. Edouard said he still might believe in ghosts because "the data points toward their existence." Data is great. Facts are great. But stories are what connect us.

And so I'm still a story collector. A word peddler. A knowledge warrior. Stories help us make sense of things that don't make sense at all. Like an unfortunate amount of bad luck. Or a forever-locked closet. Or a pile of toppled books in a deserted part of the library. I've gathered these words, these pages, this story, so I can share it with you, Friend, in hopes that you can find a bit of yourself in me or Eva or Merit or Edouard or John Jr. or Carroll. That's the truth of fiction, after all. It's hidden in feelings, not facts.

A gong sounded. Viviani capped her pen and clicked off the green library lamp, turning her warm writing circle cold and dark. And just before she headed out of the map room, Viviani knew she needed to say goodbye to one part of her story. She whispered to the whole of the New York Public Library:

"Good night, Big Red."

Viviani turned and began making her way home to where good food and good stories were waiting.

Behind her, the lamp turned back on.

Author's Note,

Dewey Decimal 809.33

see also: *authors, American; literature, modern*

Once upon a time, a girl was born in a library. Not just any library, mind you: the New York Public Library. And not just any girl: Viviani Joffre Fedeler.

That part is true, as is the fact that Viviani was named for visiting French dignitaries when her parents were stumped for a name. In fact, quite a bit of this story is true. Viviani and her brothers, John Jr. and Edouard, lived in the library with their parents because their father was the superintendent. John and Cornelia Fedeler moved into the library in July 1910, ten months before the building was opened to the public on May 23, 1911. Viviani was born there on May 8, 1917, and lived in the library for the first fifteen years of her life.

The red-bearded ghost was part of the library lore; the Fedeler children grew up hearing about the haunted stacks. And, yes, unfortunately a number of men were killed in the construction of the library itself, including a man who fell from the scaffolding while hanging plaster in the world-famous Main Reading Room. ("At least that's the way father told it," John Jr. once told the *New York Times*. It seems he knew to question John Sr.'s imaginative version of things.) The reading room has been known as the Rose Main Reading Room since the 1990s.

Viviani's papa, John H. Fedeler Sr., worked for Thomas Edison and the New York Produce Exchange, where John Jr. was born on November 12, 1906, during a power outage, and Edouard on May 13, 1908. Fedeler later became the "superintendent and consulting engineer" at the New York Public Library's flagship building on Fifth Avenue and Forty-Second Street, today known as the Stephen A. Schwarzman Building. John Sr. was an inventor, an engineer (he once "bluffed" his way into working in the chief engineer's office for the 1893 World's Fair in Chicago), a sea diver (he really did rescue "junk, metal, rifles, and the like" from shipwrecks), and a storyteller. Boy, was he a storyteller.

John Sr. would sit in his great armchair and tell his children stories, often about the red-whiskered ghost. He hoped by telling such stories that he'd cut down on the amount of late-night library exploring his children would undertake. John Sr. (not Junior, as in this tale) also told his children that the library custodian was a cannibal, with hopes that they wouldn't get underfoot when he did his rounds.

John Jr. later became the library superintendent, staying on until 1949. In his teens, he did indeed trap pigeons on the library roof (until the American Society for the Prevention of Cruelty to Animals caught wind of this and requested he free them). He and his siblings and friends later recalled many games of base-ball between the stacks, using books as bases.

And indeed, there was once a thief who tried to flee with a ten-thousand-dollar stamp collection but broke his leg in the getaway. He was found and arrested.

When the New York Public Library opened in 1911, it attracted tens of thousands of visitors on day one, including President William Howard Taft. The collection consisted of over a million volumes, largely stacked on the library's innovative seven-tiered bookshelves. The two stone lions out front are made of Tennessee marble and were originally named Leo Astor and Leo Lenox, in honor of the two private libraries that combined to make this main library. The lions are now called Patience and Fortitude.

Most of the facts about Manhattan in this story are

true, too, with two anachronistic exceptions. (*Anachronistic* is a word I think Viviani would love. . . .) There was indeed a carousel in Central Park in 1928 (there is still one there!), but it was no longer powered by a horse and donkey at that time; that "steering mechanism" ended in 1924. It was such a lovely metaphor for fiction, however—a real horse propelling fake horses—that this story collector insisted on bending time a little to include it.

Second, the type of flash Merit uses in this story wasn't widely available until 1929. Before that, flash powder was used, and as it was explosive, Merit likely wouldn't have been using it! But so much of the story takes place through Merit's lens, so I decided to keep this element in the story.

Today, the New York Public Library's stacks are largely housed underneath Bryant Park, and the process of requesting and receiving many titles is accomplished with the help of tiny "magical book trains"—a conveyor belt and small book carts (you can see them at work by visiting nypl.org/blog/2016/09/30 /magical-mystery-machine-librarians-summon-books -rose-main-reading-room). The NYPL system is made up of ninety-two branches and serves more than seventeen million patrons a year. It currently houses more than fifty-one million items. For more information about the NYPL, including photos of the many world-famous rooms mentioned in this story, visit nypl.org.

My sincerest thanks to Matthew Kirby, executive assistant to the chief external relations officer, for giving me an in-depth, behind-the-scenes tour of the Stephen A. Schwarzman Building. The library truly came alive as I saw it through Matt's eyes. Another huge thank-you to Joseph Cahalan, who also grew up as a "super's kid" in Manhattan and who endured many hours of my questions. Joe's stories of growing up in the (now demolished) Brokaw Mansion and playing after hours at the Met with his buddies added much spice and insight to Viviani's childhood. (Is it ratting you out, Joe, to let readers know that a similar version of the Master Thief game was real?!)

The moral of this story is that many amazing, sometimes hidden, things happen in a library. What's the story behind yours? What's *your* tale? The world is waiting to hear your Once Upon a Time.

≈ TIME LINE ≈

NOVEMBER 10, 1902 – The cornerstone of The New York Public
Library is laid into place on Fifth Avenue between
Fortieth and Forty-Second Streets. The cornerstone
holds a relic box containing photographs, newspapers, and letters from the era.

1902 – *Five Children and It* by E. Nesbit is first published. It hasn't
been out of print since.

NOVEMBER 12, 1906 – John Jr. is born to John and Cornelia
Fedeler at the Produce Exchange Building during a
blackout.

MAY 13, 1908 – Edouard Fedeler is born, also at the Produce
Exchange Building.

JULY 1910 – The Fedeler family moves to the library, into an
eight-room apartment on the second floor, before the
building is open to the public.

MAY 23, 1911 – The library's opening ceremony occurs, presided over by President William Howard Taft.

MAY 24, 1911 – The library opens its doors to the public. Approximately fifty thousand visitors visited the building on that first day.

1914 – World War I (then called the Great War) begins in Europe.

APRIL 6, 1917 – The United States enters World War I.

MAY 8, 1917 – Viviani Joffre Fedeler is born in the Central Building of the New York Public Library.

1918 – Many consider this year the beginning of the Harlem Renaissance, an African American cultural, social, and artistic movement anchored in New York City's Harlem neighborhood. Throughout the 1920s and '30s, influential artists like Langston Hughes and Duke Ellington shaped the movement and gained widespread exposure.

NOVEMBER 11, 1918 – World War I ends.

AUGUST 18, 1920 – The Nineteenth Amendment to the U.S. Constitution is ratified, giving women the right to vote.

1928 – *The House at Pooh Corner* by A. A. Milne is published. It would have been brand-new when Viviani and her gang used it as home plate!

MAY 20–21, 1932 – Amelia Earhart becomes the first woman to fly solo nonstop over the Atlantic Ocean.

1933 – Viviani meets and eventually marries Charles Voelker, also a building superintendent, at the annual Building Superintendent's Ball.

1941 – John Sr. retires as library superintendent. John Jr. takes on the job next.

JUNE 1949 – John Jr. resigns as the library's chief engineer.

A LOOK INTO THE LIBRARY ARCHIVES

This photograph shows the administrative offices as they would have looked when Viviani lived in the library. Doesn't it look like a tempting playground?

Viviani's bedroom window overlooked this fountain in a courtyard at the back of the building, adjacent to Bryant Park. The library's famous seven-story bookshelves were housed behind those long, thin windows to the left of the fountain. This courtyard no longer exists; it is now additional library space. This photograph was taken in 1912.

Acknowledgments

This book that you're holding right now, Friend? Lots of people helped make it the very best story it could be. Thank you:

To the team at Henry Holt Books: Lauren Bisom, Christian Trimmer, and Tiffany Liao—you are all Story Collectors Extraordinaire. Thank you, too, to the amazing Iacopo Bruno, whose beautiful artwork makes Viviani's story that much more lively and lovely.

To Josh Adams of Adams Literary, whose wisdom I value.

To Kathleen Albritton, whose research assistance was so thorough and helpful.

To Matthew Kirby, Carrie Welch, and the team at the top-notch New York Public Library. Your passion for NYPL is contagious, and your knowledge of NYPL is inspiring.

To Joe Cahalan, who let me see through the eyes of a "super's kid," and his daughter Tina Cahalan Jones. Thank you Tina, Roger, Mary Clare, and Erin for always cheering me on!

To the Goodmans, the Grishams, the Kites, the O'Donnells, and the Tubbs, especially Byron, Chloe, and Jack. You are loved more than words can say.

THE STORY CONTINUES . . .

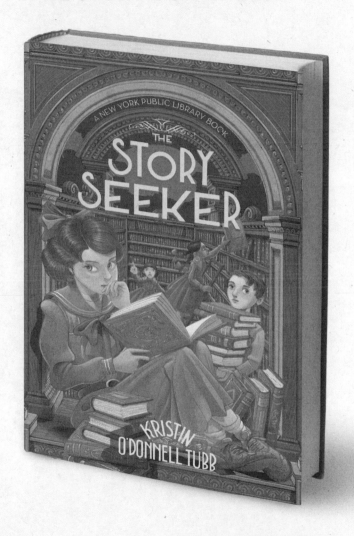

KEEP READING FOR AN EXCERPT.

CHAPTER FIVE

Fairy Tales,

Dewey Decimal 398.22

SEE ALSO: *Armenians—folklore; fairy poetry*

"I know exactly what story I'm going to write for the essay contest," Eva declared the following afternoon or they walked toward the library.

"You do?" Merit said.

Eva nodded. "It's based on an Armenian fairy tale. Want to hear it?"

"Absolutely," Viviani said quickly. She was surprised at the pang of jealousy she felt. But maybe listening to Eva's story would inspire Viviani to find hers.

"Okay." Eva took a deep breath and giggled. She was unused to having center stage. "Once there was a hen-house filled with the fattest, loudest, featheriest chickens that ever lived."

"Featheriest?" Merit asked, eyebrow raised.

Viviani elbowed her. Such a stickler, Merit could be! "Go on, Eva."

"These hens clucked and cooed and laid all sorts of beautiful, warm eggs. Brown eggs, spotted eggs—the hens were cozy and happy.

"One day, a wolf heard them gossiping, and he snuck inside the henhouse. *'Ha Ha!'* he said, teeth flashing. 'Now you will be my lunch.'

"The hens flustered and clucked, but the eldest hen puffed out her wide breast. 'If you say so,' she said. 'But first won't you please sing us a song? I understand your voice is quite lovely, and I'd regret it ever so much if I died having never heard you sing.'"

The traffic light changed, and the girls skipped across Fifth Avenue. Eva continued, breathless. "A grin crept across the wolf's wide mouth. 'A song?' he said with pride. 'Well, I suppose a farewell song couldn't hurt.' And so he sang: a deep, bellowing howl from his heart."

Eva stopped at the base of the library stairs. Up on the terrace, volunteers from the American Library Association rang large handbells as they collected used books for troops overseas. "This is not a library return box!" one of them sang cheerily. "Books for troops!"

Eva shouted over the clanging: "The wolf howled his very best songs. The mama hen's best friend, the yard dog, heard him yowling and carrying on. The dog dashed into the henhouse and chased the wolf away, taking a sizable bite out of his hindquarters."

Eva snapped her teeth with a ferocious, un-Eva-like growl, then blinked, like she'd surprised herself by telling that whole tale from memory. "The end."

Viviani and Merit laughed and applauded wildly (Viviani even whistled a little), and Eva curtsied. But as Viviani beamed at Eva, she felt a tiny twist of doubt. Eva's story was good. Could hers be that good, too? Good enough for the *Times*?

"What about you two?" Eva asked.

"I'm, er, not quite ready to share yet," Viviani blurted.

"Well, I can't wait to hear yours! How could your story not be amazing? You live in a *library*." Merit grinned. Viviani shrunk a bit, but Merit didn't seem to notice and continued, "I don't know what my story is going to be, exactly, but I know it'll be inspired by one of two photographs. Want to see them?"

"Yeah!" Viviani said a bit too loudly while Eva nodded. They followed Merit once again to the picture collection on the first floor. Mrs. Coe greeted them. Viviani thought she might live there, behind that desk. She dressed a bit old-timey, with high-neck blouses and long, full skirts. She looked like she hadn't moved from her spot in decades. Viviani had never *not* seen her there. She wondered if Mrs. Coe ever used the restroom. Or if she even ate.

Merit pulled a photograph from the Animals category. It showed a small short-haired dog and a big black-and-white cat—the duo were almost the same size—sharing a snack they'd obviously stolen from a picnic. A dirty plate lay in the grass nearby.

"Those sneaks!" Viviani said with a laugh.

Merit grinned and nodded. "You can see they've helped each other nab the food! The picture tells the whole story in a single image."

The trio of girls looked at the photo a moment longer. "Or . . . ," Merit said. She reshelved the cat-and-dog photo and pulled another photograph from the collection, this one a few rows over, from the People category.

"This one."

This photo was captioned *A Sympathetic Friend* and showed two women, both sitting, both wearing old-timey dresses, a lot like the clothes Mrs. Coe wore. One woman wore a white flower in her hair and was clasping the wrist of her friend. The friend held something—a letter?—and she touched her own face gently, as one does when truly sad, or truly deep in thought.

"Wow," breathed Eva. "What do you think is in that letter?"

"It's from the army," Viviani imagined straightaway. "Her husband died in the war."

Merit sighed. "Or it's a recipe written by her

grandmother, and this woman is remembering her *tayta* and her delicious *mahlab* bread."

Eva's fingers hovered lightly over the photo. Mrs. Coe cleared her throat, and Eva pulled her hand back. "Whatever it is, it's very important. The letter is the center of the photo. The focal point."

Merit smiled, and Viviani could see she was pleased that some of her photography lessons were sinking in.

Viviani tapped the table. "This one, Merit. You have to write about these women."

Merit looked at the image wistfully. "I think you're right."

Viviani sighed.

It is possible, Dear Friend, to feel pride and jealousy simultaneously. Viviani knew that for certain at this moment.

After eating a quick snack in the Fedeler apartment, Merit and Eva headed home. Viviani tapped a fork against her teeth, and Mama winced, turning up the radio: "Squeeze Me" by Fats Waller blasted through the jazzy airwaves.

"Mama," Viviani said, "I have to write a story for school about friendship, and I'm drawing a blank." For some reason, Viviani didn't tell her mother about the prize. Not yet. It felt like too much pressure, like a too-tight hug squeezing her ribs. She would mention it later, after she had a winning idea.

"Oh, surely not my little story collector? Storyless? Never!" Mama planted a firm kiss on the top of Viviani's red head.

Viviani knew it was meant to make her feel better. But her mother's words actually felt just like picking at that scab on her knee. Her parents were proud of her for being something she obviously was not. How could she let them down? She *had* to find a story.

"Well, where should I go for inspiration?"

Mama crossed one arm over her stomach, balanced her other elbow atop it, and rested her chin on her knuckles. "Gosh, Viviani. If I weren't so busy *living in a library*, with all those *librarians* available to *assist me*, I might be able to help you answer that question." She winked.

Viviani laughed and saluted Mama with two fingers. Mama could make her laugh even when she felt blue.

"Thanks, Mama! You're the darb!" And off Viviani dashed to find her story.

CHAPTER SIX

Curiosities and Wonders,

Dewey Decimal 032.02

SEE ALSO: *questions and answers, eccentrics and eccentricities*

Have you ever experienced a storytelling emergency? It feels rather like searching for a word that's *juuuust* on the tip of your tongue—you know the one: that valuable word that goes missing the moment you need it. That, Dear Friend, is how Viviani felt, seeking her story: like the idea was *right there*, waiting for Viviani to trip over it, capture it, bring it home, tame it, and call it her own. Her story was simply lost, hiding, and she would find it.

Viviani dashed up the stairs to the third floor and down the long, wide hallway. *Clap clap clap* went her shoes on the marble. "Slow down, Viviani!" yelled the day guard, Mr. Leon. But she couldn't slow down—this was, after all, a storytelling emergency!

She ran into the catalog room, through the grand double wooden doors, and into the Main Reading Room.

Viviani had been in this room almost every day of her life, and still, *still*, walking into it stole her breath away. Viviani's favorite part of the room was the ceiling: from it hung dozens of bronze chandeliers, each with long arms like an octopus's tentacles, holding massive globes of light. Behind the chandeliers hung a series of plaster carvings, curling and swirling and blooming like a well-tended mahogany garden. The carvings framed painted murals featuring blue skies and sunshine-rimmed clouds. They looked like windows to heaven.

The circulation desk in the Main Reading Room was a large, buttery-colored wooden beast, and three librarians buzzed around behind it. One of them was taking the book requests that library patrons had written on small scraps of paper, loaded them into metal canisters, and—*whoosh!*—sent them flying off in the vacuum of the pneumatic tubes mounted to the wall behind the desk. Viviani knew the canisters sank through the tubes and into the seven-story bookshelves just below this room. There, other librarians would pull the requested books from the miles-long stacks, then whisk them back up to the reading room in a dumbwaiter.

Whoosh! went another patron's book request. If she wrote down a wish for a story and sent it through those tubes, Viviani wondered, would her essay magically come squeaking up in the dumbwaiter?

"Hey," Viviani said to the remaining two librarians, Mr. Wilburforce and Miss Hoolihan. "I need inspiration for a homework assignment. Got any good friendship stories?"

"You'll have to be a bit more specific." Mr. Wilburforce smiled. "We're surrounded by twenty-two thousand books in this room alone!"

"You know what I mean." Viviani grinned.

Miss Hoolihan's lips thinned. "Viviani, you'll have to excuse us. We're in the middle of a crisis here."

"Crisis?" Viviani's ears perked. The best friendship stories began with a crisis! After all, the Moppets had originally teamed up to track down a missing stamp collection.

Mr. Wilburforce chuckled. "Now, hold on. I wouldn't exactly call this a crisis."

Miss Hoolihan fanned a stack of due-date cards. "Look here. Five—no, *six*—books, all of them rare medical volumes. Valuable books, these ones. *Real* valuable. All checked out on different dates, but all within days of each other. All overdue, all to the same address."

Viviani stood on tiptoe to see behind the counter. "And?"

Miss Hoolihan scowled. Honestly, one would think some of the librarians were fed a diet of lemons and sauerkraut. She spoke through flattened lips. "The name on each account is different."

Viviani still didn't understand. "And, *and*? Couldn't it just be an apartment building with a bunch of, I don't know, medical students living there or something?"

"Just what I was wondering," Mr. Wilburforce chimed in.

"Ah, but!" Miss Hoolihan said. She dug a stack of letters from a file folder. "I was just about to get to *this*. All the overdue letters we sent to that address? All came back to us this week, all marked as 'Return to Sender.' All of them say, 'No one here by that name.'"

"Okay," Viviani said. "Getting weirder." She tried to peer at the letters, but Miss Hoolihan swept them away.

"I'm going to this address tonight," Miss Hoolihan said, obviously pleased with her sleuthing skills. "I'm getting to the bottom of this."

Mr. Wilburforce smiled. "They'll turn up, I'm sure of it. Overdue books are an inconvenience to everyone, but I'd not say we're in crisis." Viviani agreed but couldn't resist the familiar tingle of a good story. Could this work as her essay? She appreciated a good mystery. She and Merit and Eva were amateur detectives, after all. They'd caught a criminal in the library just two short months ago. Boy, had that been exciting!

Viviani plopped down at a table right there and scribbled out an opening:

*Once upon a time there were missing Once Upon a Times,
and it fell to the story collector to find them.*

But when Viviani lifted her pen to write the next sentence, nothing came out. She was stumped. Sighing, she scratched through it. Nah, that wouldn't work. It made for a good mystery, but it wasn't about friendship.

"Keep me posted, Miss Hoolihan," Viviani said, looking up to where she and Mr. Wilburforce were still chatting. "And let me know if you need my help. I'm pretty good at mysteries, you know."

CHAPTER SEVEN

Tall Tales,

Dewey Decimal 398.2

SEE ALSO: *folklore, legendary characters*

At dinner that night (stewed beets—*blech!*), Edouard told the family all about the lecture he'd snuck into in the library auditorium that afternoon:

"It was about codes and codebreaking! The library has so many books on it!" The thought of using the books and resources at his very fingertips to encrypt codes had him all flustered. "Did you know that Leonardo da Vinci could *write backward*? You had to use a mirror to read it. And many folks think Shakespeare put codes in his plays. And Sir Arthur Conan Doyle wrote a whole story called "The Adventure of the Dancing Men," where Sherlock Holmes solves the murder because of a coded clue: each letter of the alphabet was represented by a dancing stick figure!"

Edouard's eyes grew wider and wider as he talked, spearing beets on his fork with gusto. "They talked about everything from the Phaistos Disc to Morse code," he continued, waving his beet-laden fork in the air. "I'm going to encrypt my next homework assignment!"

"Not sure your teachers would love that, Edouard," Mama said with a chuckle.

"Speaking of homework," Viviani mumbled around a mouthful of peas. Mama frowned. "I still need an idea. Mine all seem to have gone missing."

"For what?" Papa said.

"I need inspiration for an essay at school. I'm writing a story about friendship." Viviani quickly scooped more peas into her mouth so she didn't have to mention the prize. It simply felt *too big* if she talked about it.

Papa's face lit up. "Well, why didn't you say so?" Viviani grinned. She had come to the right place for a story.

After dinner, Papa got a hot cup of coffee and settled into his great stuffed armchair. The worn green chair was too small for Papa's large, lanky frame, but it was his favorite nonetheless. "You need a story, Viviani? Pull up a cushion, kids."

The three Fedelers scrambled to gather on the floor around Papa's chair. Mama stretched out on the couch. Story time with Papa was like watching stars glitter, like smelling roses in bloom, like splashing through the cool fountain in Bryant Park on a hot summer day. (Not that Viviani would know *anything* about that, Dear Friend. Ahem.)

"Friendship, eh?" Papa said, rubbing the stubble on his chin.

"You're friends with Thomas Edison, Papa," Edouard said. "Let's hear about him."

"Bor-*ing*," sang Viviani. "This story needs *action*. Not tinkering with inventions that don't usually work."

Papa laughed. "Action, eh? Okay, I have just the story for you. This one's about my buddy Edwin Burke, who I met in the navy."

"Yes!" John Jr. said, shifting on the floor. "I love a good raunchy sailor story."

"John Jr.," Mama said levelly.

He shrugged. "What? I do."

Viviani threw a pillow at him.

"So the *Minnesota*, that was my ship, you know. It docked in Washington. And there was this saloon there. A real dive, this place. Roaches, terrible food, watery drinks— the whole bit. It was perfect. Anyway, they were offering one hundred dollars to any man who could stand in a boxing ring for four minutes against some prizefighter."

"One hundred dollars!" Edouard said. He hugged his knees.

"Who was the boxer, Papa?" John Jr. said. "Say it was Jack Dempsey."

"Well now, that I don't recall. And here's why: no sooner had I ducked under those boxing-ring ropes than that boxer knocked me flat on my back. Out cold, I was. Huge cut over my eye, too. They dragged me out of the ring and threw a bucket of cold water in my face. I sputtered awake. Whole thing lasted maybe sixty seconds, from the ding of the bell to my ice-water bath."

At this point, Edouard and John Jr. jumped up and began acting out the story, Edouard taking a mock swing and socking John Jr.'s jaw. John spun and windmilled his arms in slow motion, taking long, heaving, exaggerated minutes to collapse in a heap. Edouard leapt about, arms overhead in a victory stance.

"What happened next, Papa? What about your buddy Edwin?" Viviani asked eagerly. Maybe this could work for her essay after all!

"He held out."

"He won the hundred dollars?" Edouard stopped leaping and returned to Papa's story in Washington.

"'Aye, there's the rub,'" Papa said, throwing in a little Shakespeare for good measure. "That rat of an owner only paid him fifty dollars."

Papa laughed, remembering it now. Edouard and John Jr. continued to box. But Viviani felt as impatient as a ticking clock. Her essay was due in less than two weeks! "What does that have to do with friendship?"

"Well, Firecracker, he used that fifty dollars to pay for my stitches!" Papa pointed to his brow—was that a faint scar, or was it really a wrinkle? He took a long swig of hot coffee. "Ah, now *that's* a good memory."

A good memory *and* a good story. One with value. Worth. Because it made everyone here smile. Would Viviani *ever* be able to tell a tale like that? This story wasn't *her* story; she couldn't use it. Plus, well, the thought of turning in a story with blood and stitches made her woozy.

Tick tick tick. Impatience swelled inside Viviani as she sat back, deep in thought. All the stories she'd heard were about friends, but they didn't capture what friendship *meant*. Viviani knew in her heart if she could capture *that*—the feeling of finding a person whose soul smiles at yours—she'd win the contest for sure.

Boy, did she wish she were like Merit or Eva—*POOF!* Idea. *POOF!* Written. They made it look easy. It left her a little grumbly, honestly.

Tick tick tick.